Treasury of Best-Loved

Children's Stories

publications international, ltd.

Contents

Contents

The Ant and the Grasshopper

A Tale of Hard Work

Adapted by Catherine McCafferty
Illustrated by Jason Wolff

Summer had just begun. Animals and insects scurried about, enjoying the summer sun. "Summer's here! The best time of the year!" the Grasshopper sang. "Warm sun, lots of fun!" he added to his song.

A line of ants marched past the Grasshopper, carrying small seeds and bits of food. As they walked along, some crumbs fell to the ground. Before the ants could get them, the Grasshopper had eaten the crumbs.

The ant at the end of the line walked up to the Grasshopper. "We've worked very hard to gather this food," said the Ant. "You should have helped us pick up what we dropped."

"That's what's wrong with your summer song," the Grasshopper sang. Then he said, "You're always working. Summertime is for play, not work."

"Summertime is for planning and gathering," said the Ant. "It's time for getting all the food we will need for the winter."

"Winter is so far away, I think I'd rather go and play," said the Grasshopper. He was about to hop off when the Ant stopped him.

"Wait! What about the food you took from us?" the Ant asked.

"Oh, yes. Thank you." The Grasshopper pointed toward a field. "And over there is a whole field of wheat to replace your crumbs. I like cornfields better myself, but that might be too far for you to walk." And the Grasshopper hopped off to the cornfield.

The Grasshopper quickly forgot about the Ant and leaped onto a cornstalk. A soft leaf gave him a bed. Above him, another leaf gave him shade. And within reach, smaller, tender leaves gave him food. There was even an ear of fresh corn nearby.

"Those ants can gather and work and store. I'll just snooze right here and snore." He fell fast asleep.

Meanwhile, the Ant lined the tunnels of his home with seeds and other foods. "When the snow is on the ground, we will be nice and warm in our nest. We will have plenty of food to eat and plenty of time to play," thought the Ant.

All that summer, the Grasshopper watched the ants. When he saw them going to a picnic for crumbs, he hopped along to eat his fill. While they carried food back to their nest, he slept in his cornstalk bed.

Then one day, the Grasshopper heard a loud noise. The farmer was coming to harvest the corn! The Grasshopper jumped into the grass. "Close call, all in all," sang the Grasshopper. "I just lost my bed and food!"

A line of ants was marching past and heard the Grasshopper. The Ant stopped. "The days are getting shorter, my friend. But there is still time for you to store food and find a winter shelter."

The Grasshopper thought about that for a second. "Not today, I've got to play," he sang and hopped his way through the grass. When he found a toadstool, he said, "This will put a roof over my head. So I'll just eat later instead."

The Grasshopper had just fallen asleep when he heard a plop! The next thing he knew, his toadstool was falling over.

"Oh, I'm sorry," chattered a squirrel above him. "My paws were so full of nuts that I dropped some. You can have them if you like."

The Grasshopper hopped away. "No, thank you. I don't like nuts, no if's, and's, or but's."

All throughout the fields and in the forests, he saw squirrels gathering nuts. They chattered to one another, "I found more!" "Have you heard? This winter is going to be snowy!" and "I have a bunch of nuts, but I want to be sure. It will be a long winter!"

All this work was making it very hard to play, and to sleep. In the hay field, the Grasshopper found a warm, sunny rock. He was just settling down, when the ants began marching by again.

"You again!" he said to the Ant. "I thought by now you'd have enough. You can't eat all that stuff!"

The Ant smiled, but he did not stop to talk. "It's always better to have a little extra than not enough," he called.

The Grasshopper frowned. The sun had moved, and the rock was cold. In the distance, the farmer was cutting hay. "Doesn't anybody here know when to play?" he asked aloud.

He hopped off to the apple orchard. Most of the leaves were gone from the tree. But the Grasshopper found a few small apples on the ground. He munched on them until he was full. Then he settled in for a nap near the root of the tree. The Grasshopper shivered. He looked around for a sunny spot, but the sun was already gone from the sky. "Someone needs to tell the sun that its working day is not done," he sang unhappily.

The sun was one thing the Grasshopper didn't mind seeing at work. With each day, though, it seemed to work less and less.

The ground seemed colder, too. One day, when the Grasshopper tried to nibble an apple, he found that it was frozen. "I don't like my apple in ice," said the Grasshopper. He was so chilly that it was hard to think of a second line to his rhyme. "Ice, nice, rice, mice. . . ."

The Grasshopper tried to think of something nice. "A warm place with lots of rice," he sang in a shivery voice. He didn't really like rice, but he was getting hungry. Then he thought, "Maybe I'll visit my friends, the mice." The Grasshopper crept into the home of the field mouse family. It was warm inside. There was no sign of rice, but the Grasshopper was sure they would have something else nice.

"Thank you for visiting, Mr. Grasshopper," said Mother Mouse. "I would invite you to stay, but all of my sisters and brothers are moving in for the winter. Isn't that nice? Oh, here they are now!"

A crowd of mice rushed into the nest. It was nice to see them hugging each other. But the Grasshopper wanted the kind of nice that meant he had a place to live and something to eat. He was out of luck at the Mouse house.

The Grasshopper hopped back to the orchard. The ground was so cold that it hurt his tiny feet. "Where are those ants, now that I need them?" sang the Grasshopper.

Suddenly snow began to fall. It covered the Grasshopper. With a jump, he fluttered his wings.

He had to get inside or he would freeze! Hopping as fast as he could, the Grasshopper raced to the Ant's home. "Is anybody home?" he called as he stepped into the tunnels.

"Why aren't you out playing in the snow?" asked the wise Ant.

The Grasshopper wanted to say that he had just come by for a visit. But he could feel the cold wind on his back. Sadly, the Grasshopper sang, "I should have listened to what you said. Now I'm cold and scared and unfed." It wasn't his best song, but he hoped the Ant would understand.

The Ant did understand. But he wanted to be sure that the Grasshopper understood, too. "We got our food for the winter by working hard. If you stay with us this winter, you'll have to work hard, too."

The Grasshopper gulped. What if it was a long winter, like the one squirrel said? But then he remembered the ice and snow.

"Your job here will be to sing for us. Every day." Then the Ant laughed. "Because winter is our time to play."

All that winter, the Grasshopper sang for the Ant and his huge family. And the next summer, the Grasshopper sang a song as he helped to gather food. "Summer work is slow and steady. But when winter comes, I'll be ready!"

Hard Work

The ants' hard work pays off when winter comes. The Grasshopper, who plays all summer, has no food when the weather gets colder. The Grasshopper sees the ants' work as no fun, but the Grasshopper soon learns that it is no fun to be cold and hungry, either.

Putting off things that you don't want to do is easy. After you play a game, playing another game without putting the first one away is easy. Nevertheless, when too many toys are out at once, they can get lost or broken. Putting away your toys after you play with them keeps them nice and ready for the next time you want to play. Now that's fun!

The Twelve Dancing Princesses

A Tale of Kindness

Adapted by Sarah Toast

Illustrated by Pamela R. Levy

Long ago there lived a king who had twelve beautiful and clever daughters. The princesses all slept in the same huge room, with their twelve pretty beds in a row.

The king loved his daughters, but he was becoming concerned about what they did each night. Even though the king carefully locked the door of the princesses' room every night, the next morning he found the princesses tired and out of sorts. More puzzling still, their tiny silk dancing slippers were worn to shreds. Every day, the king had to order twelve new pairs of silk shoes for his daughters.

The next morning, when the king begged his daughters to explain why they were so tired and pale, and why their dancing shoes were in shreds, the princesses merely murmured, "Beloved Papa, we have been sleeping peacefully in our beds all night."

The king thought of a way to find out the truth. He issued a proclamation declaring that the first man to solve the mystery of where the twelve princesses went to dance every night would choose a wife from among them. However, anyone who tried to discover the princesses' secret had only three days and three nights to succeed.

It was not long before a prince arrived at the palace to try his luck. The king made the young prince feel welcome. The prince was led to a small chamber next to the princesses' bedroom. The door between the two rooms was left open. The princesses could not leave without being seen by the prince.

When the princesses filed into their room, the prince gladly accepted a cup of wine offered to him by the eldest princess. In no time, he was sound asleep in his bed.

When the prince awoke the next morning, the princesses were asleep in their beds. The prince was dismayed to see twelve pairs of worn-out shoes!

The next two nights, the same thing happened. The king was angry and banished the prince from the kingdom.

Many other princes met the same fate. The king began to despair of ever finding out where his daughters danced at night.

Then one day a poor soldier came limping along the road. He had been wounded and could no longer serve in battle. He had no sooner sat down by the side of the road to eat some bread and cheese when an old woman appeared all dressed in rags.

"Won't you have a bite to eat with me?" said the kind soldier to the woman. He offered her half of his simple meal.

"Where are you going?" asked the woman.

"I am going to the city to find work," replied the soldier. "Perhaps I can find out how the princesses wear out their shoes!"

The old woman surprised the soldier by saying, "Heed my words! Do not drink the wine that the princesses offer you. Pretend to fall asleep. And take this cloak, which will make you invisible. You can follow the princesses and discover their secret!"

The soldier didn't know what to think. He thanked the old woman and continued on his way. The soldier put on the cloak and discovered that it did indeed make him invisible. He headed at once to the king's palace, where he was made welcome.

In the evening, the soldier was led to the little room next to the princesses' bedroom. Soon the eldest princess brought the soldier a cup of wine. He pretended to drink the wine, letting it trickle down into his scarf. Then he pretended to fall asleep.

When the eldest princess heard the soldier's snores, she quietly said to her sisters, "He is as foolish as the others. Make haste. We must get ready for the ball!"

The twelve princesses chattered and laughed as they dressed in their best ball gowns and jewels and arranged each other's hair. Only the youngest princess felt uneasy. "Something just doesn't feel right tonight," she said.

"Don't be such a little goose," said the eldest princess fondly. "That soldier is sound asleep. He won't wake up until morning!"

When the princesses were ready, they put on their dancing shoes. Then the eldest princess tapped on her bedpost three times. The bed sank into the floor and became a long staircase.

The eldest princess stepped down into the opening in the floor. One by one, her sisters followed her.

The soldier sprang out of bed and threw on the cloak. Then he followed the youngest princess down the stairway.

Because his leg was lame, the soldier stumbled and stepped on the hem of the youngest princess's gown. She shrieked with alarm.

The princesses and the soldier continued down many flights of stairs until at last they came to a forest of marvelous silver trees. Then they came across trees of gold and trees of diamonds. As they passed each forest, the soldier reached up and broke off a branch from each kind of tree. Every time a branch cracked, the youngest princess cried out. And every time, the eldest princess reassured her that there was nothing to worry about.

The twelve princesses hurried to the edge of a beautiful lake. There, twelve princes awaited them in twelve little painted boats. Each princess took the hand of a handsome prince.

The soldier quickly hopped into the boat with the youngest princess and her companion.

On the other side of the lake stood a splendid castle. As the beautiful little boats approached the castle, a fanfare of trumpets announced the arrival of the twelve princesses and fireworks lit up the sky.

The princes and the princesses stepped into the castle, where beautiful music welcomed them to the ballroom. The princesses danced with their princes for half the night.

Soon the princesses' slippers were worn out. The princes rowed the twelve princesses back across the lake, and this time the soldier rode with the eldest sister. The princesses bade their princes good-bye and promised to return the next night. Then the princesses hurried back the way they had come.

The princesses were so tired that they slowed down at the top of the last set of stairs. The soldier was able to dash ahead of them, throw off his cloak, and jump into his bed.

The princesses dragged themselves into their room and put their worn and tattered shoes in a row. The eldest princess checked on the soldier to be sure he was asleep and said to her sisters, "We are safe!" With that, all twelve sisters fell fast asleep.

The soldier wanted to see the forests and the castle again, so he followed the princesses the next night and the next. The third night, the soldier took a golden cup from the castle to show the king as proof.

The next morning the king sent for the soldier and asked him, "Good soldier, have you discovered where my daughters dance their shoes to shreds every night?"

"Your Highness, I have," said the soldier. "They sneak down a hidden staircase. Then they walk through three enchanted forests to a beautiful lake. Twelve princes take them across the lake to a castle where they dance the night away."

The king couldn't believe the soldier's story until the soldier showed him the golden cup and the branches of silver, gold, and diamonds. The king called his daughters, who admitted the truth.

The king told the soldier to choose one of the princesses to be his wife. The soldier had already decided that he liked the eldest princess best. She was clever and spirited as well as beautiful. For her part, the princess thought the soldier was clever and kind.

The soldier was given royal garments to wear. He and the eldest princess were married, and the wedding guests happily danced the night away.

Kindness

The poor soldier was kind to the old woman, who was a stranger to him. In return, she helped him solve the mystery of the twelve dancing princesses. The soldier didn't have much food, but he shared with the woman anyway. He did not expect a reward for his kindness and the woman did not seem wealthy. The soldier knew that sharing his food was the right thing to do. He knew that kindness is its own reward.

Have you ever done something nice for someone? Did it give you a good feeling to do something nice? Did you expect a reward for your good deed?

The Brave Little Tailor

A Tale of Ingenuity

Adapted by Jennifer Boudart
Illustrated by Jeremy Tugeau

One morning, a little tailor sat in his shop. He bent over his work, sewing as he always did this time of day. Suddenly the tailor had a taste for raspberry jelly. He took out a loaf of bread, and cut a big slice from it. The tailor licked his lips as he spread on some jelly. "I am more hungry than I thought," he told himself. "I sure hope this jelly fills my belly and clears my head."

The tailor wanted to sew a few more stitches before eating his snack. When he finished, he saw a swarm of flies buzzing around his tasty jelly. The little man waved the flies away with his hand. But they flew right back.

The tailor grabbed a scrap of cloth and growled, "Now I'll let you have it!" The cloth burst through the air as the tailor beat at the buzzing flies.

When he lifted the cloth away, seven flies lay dead on the table. "The whole world should know of my skill!" said the tailor. He cut a belt just his size. With his finest thread, he sewed these words: "Seven in one blow!" The tailor tied the red belt around his waist. "I feel the need for a big adventure!" he shouted.

The tailor looked for something useful to take with him on his big adventure. All he found was an old piece of cheese. He put it in his pocket. As he was locking the door, he heard a rustle in the bushes. A bird was trapped among the thorns. The tailor gently pulled the bird from the bush. He put it in his pocket with the cheese. Then he set off to find adventure.

The tailor walked through town and up the side of a mountain. At the top, he met a giant. "Hello, Giant," said the tailor with a bow. "I am on a big adventure. Will you join me?"

"A little man like you on a big adventure?" rumbled the giant. For an answer, the tailor showed the giant his belt. The giant read the words: "Seven in one blow!"

The giant, who was not very smart, thought that the belt meant seven men, not flies. He found it very hard to believe that this tiny tailor could kill seven men with one blow. So he decided to test the man's strength. "You must be very strong. Can you do this?" asked the giant. He picked up a stone and squeezed it until water dripped from the stone.

The tailor was obviously not as strong as the giant, but he was much more clever. "Watch this," the little tailor said as he took something from his pocket. The giant thought it was a stone, too, but it was actually the piece of cheese. The tailor squeezed it in his hand until liquid whey dripped from his palm.

The giant raised his eyebrows. "Well, can you do this?" he asked. He picked up another stone and tossed it high into the air. It flew almost out of sight.

"Watch this," the tailor said as he took something from his pocket. It was the bird, of course. With a toss of his hand, the tailor sent the little bird flying. Pretty soon the bird was out of sight. In fact, it never came down!

This did not convince the giant, though. He was a poor loser. "If you are so strong, help me carry this tree," the giant ordered.

Once again, the tailor knew he was not as strong as the giant. He quickly came up with an idea. The tailor walked to the leafy end of the fallen oak. "I will carry the branches," he said. "I wouldn't want them to scratch you. Besides, it is no trouble for one who can kill seven at one blow."

The giant lifted the tree trunk onto his shoulder. He could not see the tailor at the other end. The tailor knew this. He hopped into the branches and let the giant do all the work. When the giant stopped to rest, the tailor jumped out and pretended to be carrying the leafy end of the tree. When the giant looked back at the tailor, he saw that he was not even tired!

"Perhaps you would like to come home with me and meet my friends," the giant said with an evil gleam in his eye.

"Certainly," the clever tailor replied.

The giant took the tailor to his cave. A group of giants sat around a roaring fire. They watched as their friend led the little man into the cave. "You can sleep here," said the giant pointing to a giant-size bed. "Even a man who can kill seven in one blow needs to rest!"

The tailor was not used to sleeping in such a big bed. So he slept in a corner instead. It was good for him that he did. During the night, the giants pounded on the bed with clubs, until they thought they had taken care of the pesky tailor.

In the morning, the giants went swimming in the river. They joked about the strange man and his silly belt. When the tailor walked up whistling a merry tune, the giants were so afraid, they ran away without their clothes! The tailor laughed and left the giants behind. He walked very far and then lay down for a nap.

As the tailor slept, some people found him and read his belt. They thought he was a mighty soldier and took him to meet their king. The king was impressed and hired him for his army. He also gave him a bag full of gold.

But the other soldiers were angry at this new soldier.

"This is not fair!" they told the king. "We will leave your army if we don't get a bag full of gold, too."

The king could not lose his whole army. He decided to get rid of his new soldier. He went to the little man with a challenge. "I need you to kill two giants that live in my woods. If you do, I will give you my daughter and half my kingdom as a reward."

The tailor knew this was his chance to become a hero.

The next morning, the tailor rode off to find the giants with one hundred soldiers behind him and a brilliant plan. "Stay behind until I call you," he told the soldiers at the edge of the woods.

The tailor found the two giants asleep under a tree. He climbed the tree and began dropping acorns on one giant's head. The giant awoke and turned to his friend. "Why did you wake me by thumping my head?" roared the giant.

Before his friend could answer, the angry giant threw an acorn at him. The two giants fought each other until both fell dead. The tailor called the king's soldiers to see what he had done. They were amazed. The new soldier had not even a scratch!

"Two giants are easy. Try seven in one blow," said the tailor.

The king heard about the tailor's great feat, but didn't want to give up his daughter and half his riches, yet. He ordered him to catch a unicorn that was scaring the villagers. The tailor agreed to go, but only if he could go alone. The king agreed. So, off to the woods the tailor went looking for the unicorn.

Suddenly, the tailor turned to see the unicorn running straight for him. He stood perfectly still. Just as the unicorn reached him, the tailor jumped out of the way. He had been standing in front of a tree. The unicorn's horn stuck fast into the tree's hard wood.

The tailor freed the unicorn and rode it back to the palace in a cloud of dust. Again the king was amazed to see the tailor.

The king had no choice but to keep his promise. He could not prove that the man who married his daughter and took half his kingdom was nothing but a hero.

The tailor almost gave up his secret one night, though. While he was sleeping, his new wife heard him say, "This new fabric will make a fine waistcoat."

The princess leapt out of bed and hid behind a curtain, hoping her husband would reveal more of his true identity.

But the clever tailor, wakened by his wife's movement, quickly realized what he had said in his sleep. "I mean, a prince and a man who can kill seven with one blow should have the finest waistcoat around. Right?"

Ingenuity

The tailor was not big or strong, but he was very clever. The little tailor used his wits to defeat the giants and win the hand of the princess. He knew that the giants weren't very smart and could be easily fooled. He used his brain again to capture the unicorn for the king. He proved that you don't have to be a giant to be a giant-size hero!

Sometimes a small person will surprise you with a big heart or big ideas. Have you ever thought you knew what a person was like, and then they did something completely unexpected? Have you ever used your own ingenuity when up against a bully?

The City Mouse and the Country Mouse

A Tale of Appreciation

Adapted by Lisa Harkrader

Illustrated by Dominic Catalano

Once upon a time a country mouse named Oliver lived in a hole under the root of a big old oak tree. Oliver loved the sound of squirrels chattering during the day and crickets chirping at night. He loved the smell of rich dirt and hearty grass all around him.

One day Oliver invited his city cousin, Alistair, for a visit. Before Alistair arrived, Oliver tidied up his hole. He straightened his oak leaf bed. He spread fresh pine needles on the floor. He scrubbed the tuna can table and polished the bottle cap plates. Then Oliver sat by the entrance to his hole, gazed out at the stars, and waited for his cousin Alistair to arrive.

When Alistair arrived, he set his fine leather suitcase on the pine needles. "I say, cousin, is this your cellar?" he asked Oliver.

"No," said Oliver, "it's my home."

Oliver showed Alistair the back of the hole, where he stored his grain. He led Alistair up onto the nob of the old oak root, where he sometimes sat to watch the sunset. Then he sat Alistair down at the tuna can table and served him a dinner of barleycorn and wheat germ.

Alistair nibbled his meal politely. "This certainly tastes as though it's good for me." He coughed and swallowed. "A bit dry, perhaps. Could I bother you for a cup of tea?"

Oliver brewed up a thimble of dandelion tea for them both. "Here's to my cousin Alistair! Thanks for visiting," toasted Oliver.

When the thimbles were empty, Oliver changed into his long johns, Alistair changed into his silk pajamas, and the mice settled into their oak leaves for the night. After Alistair rustled around in his oak leaves for a while, he finally drifted off to sleep.

Oliver awoke early the next morning, as usual. A robin family twittered in the old oak tree. A rooster crowed at a nearby farm.

Alistair squeezed his pillow over his ears. "Oh, dear. What is that confounded racket?" he mumbled.

"That's the sound of morning in the country," said Oliver. "It's the wonderful music that makes me want to start the new day."

Alistair pulled the pillow from his face and opened one eye. "You start your day in the morning?" he asked.

"Here in the country we rise at dawn," Oliver said, buttoning his overalls. He pulled on his sturdy work boots and pushed his wheelbarrow out into the morning sun.

Alistair rolled to the edge of his oak leaf bed. He wiped the sleep from his eyes. He slid his feet into his shiny black dress shoes and followed his cousin outside.

Oliver gathered acorns and stacked them near his hole. Then he shucked the seeds from the tall rye grass and carried them into the hole. Then he went to the cornfield to find fallen corn.

While Oliver was hard at work, Alistair yawned and leaned against the root of the old oak tree. Then he wiped the dust from his shoes with his silk handkerchief.

When Oliver returned with some corn, he piled it neatly.

"Thank goodness you're done." Alistair collapsed into the wheelbarrow. "Now I'd say it's time for a snack and a nap."

Oliver giggled. "The work isn't finished. We still have lots to do before we can rest."

Alistair sighed. "I'm simply not cut out for the country life," he said. "A mouse could starve to death here. Come home with me for a while. I'll show you the good life."

Alistair packed his silk pajamas into his fine leather suitcase. Oliver packed his long johns into his beat-up carpet bag. The two mice set out for Alistair's home in the city.

Oliver followed Alistair over fields and valleys, into dark, noisy subway tunnels, and through crowded city streets until they reached the luxury hotel where Alistair lived.

Alistair stopped in front of the door. "Polished marble floors and shiny brass knobs," he said. "Now, this is how mice like us are supposed to live."

Oliver stared up at the revolving glass door. "H-h-how do we get inside, Alistair?"

"Wait till the opening comes around, then run through," Alistair replied. The door swung around, and Alistair disappeared inside. It took a few more spins before Oliver gave it a try.

Oliver whirled around and around in the revolving door until Alistair tugged Oliver's carpet bag and dragged him inside.

Oliver followed Alistair across the lobby and through a small crack in the wall hidden by velvet draperies.

"My apartment," Alistair said when they were inside.

Oliver looked around in amazement. Alistair's home was filled with gold candlesticks, crystal goblets, and linen napkins.

"We're under the bandstand." Alistair pointed out the hole that was his front door. "An orchestra plays, and ladies and gentlemen dance every night until dawn."

"How can you sleep with all the noise?" asked Oliver.

"Sleep?" said Alistair. "I can sleep during the day. We do things a little differently here. Dinner, for example. At a five-star hotel, dinner begins with hors d'oeuvres."

Alistair led Oliver through the dining room. They hid behind potted plants and raced under tablecloths. They waited until the chef went to check something in the dining room, then they scampered across the kitchen and into the dark pantry where Oliver stumbled over something.

"Do be careful," said Alistair.

Oliver saw what he'd stumbled over. "It's a-a-a . . ."

"A mousetrap." Alistair scooted it under a shelf with his paw. "You'll learn to stay away from them."

Alistair led Oliver up the shelves to the hors d'oeuvres. Alistair gobbled fancy crackers, nibbled pasta, and even managed to chew a hole in a tin of smoked salmon.

"Now this," said Alistair, patting his tummy, "is fine dining."

Oliver was still so frightened, that he barely ate a crumb.

"Tonight the chef is preparing roast duck with herbed potatoes in a delicate cream sauce." Alistair's mouth watered. His whiskers twitched. "One taste and you'll never go back to the country."

The mice crept out of the pantry. The kitchen seemed empty. Alistair darted about, gathering up bits of duckling and potatoes. He didn't notice the chef marching back into the kitchen.

But the chef noticed Alistair. "You again!" shouted the chef. The chef chased the mice around the kitchen with a broom.

Alistair and Oliver escaped through a hole under the sink.

"No main course tonight, I'm afraid," said Alistair. "But don't worry, cousin. We'll make up for it with dessert."

Alistair showed Oliver the tarts and turnovers and cheesecakes. Oliver timidly nibbled the edge of a flaky cream puff. It was so delicious! He leaned forward to get a bigger bite and splat!

The cart lurched forward. Oliver had landed face down in the cream puff. Alistair grabbed the edge of a lacy napkin and hung on tight as a waiter wheeled the cart across the dining room.

Oliver wobbled off the cart. "I'm not cut out for life in the city," he said. "You take too many risks for your dinner. A mouse could starve to death here, too. I'm going home to the good life."

So Oliver dragged his carpet bag back through crowded city streets, over fields and valleys until he reached his hole under the root of the big old oak tree.

He ate a late supper of acorns and wheat kernels, then curled up in his oak leaf bed. He could hear the crickets chirping.

Back at his hotel, Alistair curled up in his linen napkin and listened to the orchestra play.

Both mice sighed. "I love being home," they said.

Appreciation

The two mice realized that there is no place like home! They learned to appreciate the life they have. The city mouse was not happy living in the country and the country mouse was not happy living in the city. Neither home was better than the other, but each mouse was happy in his own home.

Have you ever stayed at a friend's house and noticed that things seemed strange or different from your house? That doesn't mean that your friend's house is not as good as yours. You are probably more comfortable in your own home, with your family and your own toys. This means that you appreciate what you have.

Saint George and the Dragon

A Tale of Courage

Adapted by Brian Conway

Illustrated by Tammie Lyon

This is the tale of St. George and the dragon. It has been told for over 15 centuries. It takes place during a time called the Dark Ages, when kings ruled the land, wizards cast spells, and monsters roamed free.

The queen of fairies had taken young George in as a baby. The fairies raised the child to grow up brave, strong, calm, courteous, quick, and clever. They taught him to be a noble knight.

At last the time came when George was old enough to seek out his destiny. The queen of fairies called him to see her.

"Your journey starts today," she told him. "You have many adventures before you. Your fantastic quest will take six years. The world is filled with monsters to be slain and battles to be fought. You'll meet kings and paupers, wizards and witches, evil princes and kind princesses."

"Yes, Your Majesty," George bowed before the queen. He was very fond of her. He was sad to leave the land of the fairies, but he was not afraid.

"Always remember one thing," the queen added, tapping George's silver battle helmet. "Your greatest weapon, George, is your brain."

With those words, George set off. He traveled for weeks, through many wonderful kingdoms. But as George approached Silene, he noticed the land changed from lush and green to dark and desolate. It seemed the ground had been crossed by fire. There was no grass, only the darkest mud. The trees were bare and black, and a foul stench filled the air.

As George walked through this stark land, he did not see a soul—not a bird, not a squirrel, and certainly not a single person.

George finally saw a castle in the distance. A high, solid wall enclosed the castle and the small city around it. The gate was closed up tight. Again, George saw no one around. When he got closer, he saw a young lady. She crept quietly through the gate.

"Excuse me, my dear lady," he called after her.

"Quiet!" she hushed him. "Have you no sense? You would do well to leave here now and never return."

"But I am a brave knight here to help you," George whispered.

"Alas, sir," the woman replied, "you are but one man. I fear that you cannot help."

George looked her in the eyes. "It is my destiny," he said to her. "I will not go until I have done all I can, even if it costs me my life."

"I am Princess Sabra," she said. "Come with me."

They tiptoed through what was once a deep, green forest. Sabra explained why the kingdom lived in such fear.

A fearful dragon had lived in the kingdom for many years, she told him. The horrible beast had ravaged the land. Many men had tried to slay the dragon, but its sharp claws, vast flapping wings, and fiery breath made it impossible to reach, let alone kill.

The people had moved to protection within the castle walls. But soon the dragon had run out of animals to eat.

"If you do not feed me sheep each day," the dragon roared, "I will come through those walls for my breakfast!" So each day, as the sun rose, so rose the dragon, looking for its breakfast.

"The dragon sleeps now," said the princess, "but we gave up our last two sheep this very morning. Tomorrow we shall have nothing to give the dragon, and we shall all perish."

"Then I have arrived at the right time," said George bravely.

They came to a cave in the dark forest. "To slay the dragon," Sabra told George, "we need help. That is why we are here."

In the cave there lived a wise old hermit. Some said he was a sorcerer over 900 years old, but no one knew for sure.

Sabra and George crept up to the hermit, who stared into his fire. He did not turn to look at them, but he spoke as if he knew they were coming.

Long ago, it was told,
Two brave knights would come to know,
The only way to save the rest:
The Serpent's weakness in his breath.

With those words, an ancient hourglass appeared at their feet. George did not understand. He asked the strange little man, but the hermit would speak no more.

When George and Sabra left the cave, it was already dark. They knew they must hurry to the dragon's lair. They had to get there while the dragon slept.

"The hermit speaks in puzzles," Sabra sighed. "What do we do with this ancient timepiece?"

George remembered what the queen of fairies had told him. His best weapon, she had said, was his brain. He studied the hourglass closely. Each bit of sand looked like a magic crystal frozen in time.

They arrived at the lake. George and Sabra walked softly through the fog so they would not be heard. The sands in the hourglass dropped with every careful step.

"The hourglass will lead us," George whispered. "We must wait until all the sand has dropped through."

The smell as they approached the lair was horrible. George and the princess set George's shield near the sleeping dragon's head to protect themselves from the dragon's fiery snores. They watched the icy blue sands tick away.

Suddenly the dragon stirred. Now Sabra thought, surely the dragon would find them before all the sands ran through the hourglass. The dragon raised up and rubbed his slimy eyes.

As George watched the dragon rise, he stopped watching the hourglass! The very last grain of sand was dropping through. At that moment, the dragon yawned a great, fiery yawn.

"Now, George!" Sabra shouted.

George knew what to do. He threw the hourglass up into the dragon's yawning mouth. It shattered on the dragon's slithering tongue in a cloud of icy mist.

Now our two heroes had sorely angered the dragon. He looked down to see them. Both George and Sabra ducked behind the shield. The dragon reared back to hurl a fiery blast at them. But, as fortune would have it, only cool ice and soft snow came from the dragon's mouth. The dragon took a deep breath, certain the furnace inside of him would melt the ice.

But, the hermit's magic had changed the dragon. His mouth shut tight with frozen ice, the once-fearsome dragon jumped into the deep, warm lake. Only there could he keep from freezing from the inside out.

That dragon never bothered another soul. Some have seen him coming up for air on occasion, but only on very warm nights. The dragon would not dare stay out of the warm water too long, for fear of becoming a giant icy statue.

George and Sabra had saved the kingdom. It was Sabra who was the second knight that the old Hermit had spoke of in his strange riddle.

The two arrived at the castle to great cries of joy and triumph. The grateful people of Silene were no longer prisoners in their own kingdom.

The king offered George all he had in thanks, but George wanted no payment for his deeds.

"I have many more adventures left to face," George told the people. "They are my greatest reward."

George shared the story of the dragon of Silene to whomever asked along his journey. And it is still told today as an example of bravery and good versus evil. That is how George, the brave knight from the land of the fairies, earned his sainthood.

Courage

When George agreed to fight the dragon, he did not think of the danger that might come to him. He thought only of saving other people from the dragon's danger. George faced this danger without thinking of himself. He was truly brave.

Being brave can be a very hard thing to do, but there are lots of ways to show courage. Meeting new people can be a very scary thing and is a good opportunity to show how brave you can be. If you smile and say "Hello," chances are the new person will be happy that you did, and he or she will smile back. It takes a really courageous person to smile first.

The Golden Goose

A Tale of Generosity

Adapted by Brian Conway
Illustrated by Karen Dugan

There once was a gentle boy called Samuel. He lived at the edge of the forest with his parents and two older brothers. His family often treated him poorly. They didn't know that he was capable of much greater things, until the day he met a strange old man in the woods.

That day began as Samuel's oldest brother went to cut wood. Their mother packed a nice sweet cake and a bottle of cider for her oldest son to take into the woods. Samuel stayed home and chopped nuts.

In the woods, Samuel's brother came upon a little gray man.

The man kindly bid him good day and said, "Will you share your meal with a tired old man? I am very hungry and thirsty."

Samuel's brother yelled at the man. "If I share with you, I won't have enough for myself," he said. "Now out of my way!"

The brother left the man standing there and went to chop a tree. After a few strong swings, his ax slipped and hit his arm. He suffered a deep cut and could no longer continue his work. The little man saw all this happen. He smiled as the oldest brother hurried home to dress his wound.

Now the second brother was called to get the firewood. Their mother gave him sweet cake and cider for his journey, as she'd done for the oldest brother. Before long the second brother also met up with the old man in the woods.

The man kindly bid him good day and said, "Would you share your meal with a tired old man? I am very hungry and thirsty."

This next brother was as selfish as the first. "If I give you my food and drink, I won't have enough for myself," he said. "Now get out of my way!"

The second brother walked away and found a tree to chop. He swung so strongly with his ax, the head of the ax dropped off. It fell firmly on the brother's foot, and he, too, could no longer work. Again the little gray man smiled as he watched Samuel's second brother hobbling home.

Then young Samuel said, "Let me go cut the wood, Father."

"You know nothing about it," his father replied harshly. "But if you are so willing to get hurt, then go."

Samuel's mother handed him some stale bread and a jug of warm water and sent him on his way. In the forest, Samuel met the little gray man as well.

The old man kindly bid him good day and said, "Would you share some food and drink with a tired old man? I am so very hungry and thirsty."

"I have only stale bread and warm water," Samuel said, "but if you don't mind that, we can eat together."

They sat in the woods to eat. When Samuel reached for their snack, he found a magnificent sweet cake and a large bottle of cider for them to share.

"My, look at this," said Samuel. "I am glad I have much more than stale bread to share with you."

When they finished their tasty meal, the old man told Samuel, "You shared your goods with me, and for that I am grateful. Now you will have good luck to go with your kind heart."

The little gray man pointed at an old tree nearby. "Cut down that tree and you'll find something special there in its roots." Then the man walked away without another word.

Samuel was puzzled, but did as the old man said.

Samuel raised his ax and swiftly cut down the old tree. When the tree fell, more than just a stump remained! Samuel found a goose sitting among the roots. This was no ordinary goose. Its feathers were made of gold!

"What a wonderful surprise!" shouted Samuel.

Samuel had never seen such a splendid sight before! He picked up the goose. Sure enough, its feathers were pure gold! Samuel took the goose and hurried into town. He had to show this great goose to everyone he knew.

Samuel beamed proudly as he carried his golden goose through the town. He passed an inn, and the innkeeper's three curious daughters came out to see the beautiful bird. Each of the three daughters wanted to take one of the goose's golden feathers to keep for her own.

When Samuel stopped to show off the golden goose to the three sisters, the oldest sister tiptoed behind Samuel and tugged at the goose's wing. Her hand stuck there so tightly that she could not move it away. She waved to her sisters for their help.

The sisters thought that together they could surely pluck out three gold feathers! They joined hands to pull. Instead, the three sisters found they were all stuck to each other! The sisters hushed their worried squeals and scurried behind Samuel, who never noticed the girls hanging on behind. He marched for the next town to share his goose's beauty with anyone who wished to behold it.

Samuel hurried through a field on his way to the next town. The three stuck girls followed closely behind. In the field, he passed a minister and his wife.

The minister saw the odd procession and cried out at the three sisters, "Have you no shame, girls? Why must you run after the boy? It's just not proper!"

The minister tried to pull the youngest girl away. All too soon he felt that he himself was stuck, and he had to run as fast as his legs could carry him to keep up with the others.

The minister's wife saw her husband running along with the three girls. She cried out in amazement, "Dear Husband, slow down! We have to be at a wedding in a few minutes!"

The minister's wife pulled on his sleeve. Then she was caught up in this silly parade, too.

They passed two farmers on a road. The minister's wife called for help, but as soon as they touched her, the farmers were pulled along, too!

Samuel hurried into the next town, with the curious party of seven behind him. There a king lived with his only daughter. The princess was so serious and solemn that it was believed she could not laugh. So the king sent out a proclamation. Whoever made the princess laugh would have her hand in marriage.

When Samuel heard about the princess, he took his golden goose to her. At the sight of this bumbling parade, the princess burst into fits of laughter. The king thought she might not stop.

Samuel asked the princess to marry him. But before she could answer, the king stepped in. He did not want Samuel to marry his daughter, so he made up a list of conditions for Samuel.

"First," the king said, "bring me a man who can drink a whole cellarful of cider, then a man who can eat a mountain of bread."

Samuel thought of the little man in the woods and rushed off.

The old man was sitting in the same spot as before. "Oh, I'm so thirsty and so very hungry," said the man to Samuel. "I cannot seem to drink enough cider or eat enough bread."

Samuel quickly took the old man to see the king. The little man happily drank all the cider and ate all the bread in the king's cellar. Then Samuel approached the king and asked for his bride.

But the king was ready with a third demand. "Now bring me a ship which sails on land as well as at sea." Again, Samuel went to see the little man.

"I will share all my magic with you," said the old man, "because you have been so kind to me."

Soon Samuel was back at the castle with a ship that sailed on land and sea. The king had no choice but to let Samuel marry the princess. The two were married that very day.

Generosity

The boy in the story, Samuel, did not get the same kind of treatment from his parents as his brothers did, and yet he was very generous with his meal when approached by the old man. He realized that sharing what little he had was better than letting this old man go hungry. Because the boy was so generous, the man rewarded him with wonderful gifts and kindness.

Being generous and doing kind things for people will not always be rewarded with favors or special gifts. Nevertheless, a feeling of making someone happy in a time of need is, in itself, a reward.

Demeter and Persephone

A Tale of Love

Adapted by Megan Musgrave
Illustrated by Michael Jaroszko

125

Hades, the king of the Underworld, sat on his lonely throne one day and wished that something could make his world a nicer place to live. The Underworld was cold and dark and dreary, and the sun never shined there. No one ever came to visit Hades because the gates of the Underworld were guarded by Cerberus, a huge three-headed dog. Cerberus looked so fierce that he scared everyone away.

It made Hades very grumpy to be the king of such a cold and lonely world. "I need a companion who will bring joy to this dark, dreary place," said Hades. This gave Hades an idea. He decided to disguise himself as a poor, lonely traveler and go up to the earth's surface. There he would be able to find a companion. He would find someone who could help him make the Underworld a happier place to live.

Upon the earth lived Demeter, the goddess of the harvest. Demeter had a beautiful daughter named Persephone. Persephone had long, golden hair and rosy cheeks, and happiness followed her wherever she went. Demeter loved her daughter very much, and she was always full of joy when Persephone was near.

When the goddess of the harvest was happy, the whole world bloomed with life. The fields and orchards were always full of crops to be harvested.

Persephone loved to run through the fields and help Demeter gather food for the people of the earth. But best of all, she loved to play in the apple orchards. There, she could climb the apple trees and pick large, juicy apples to eat.

When Hades was visiting the earth, he saw Persephone playing in an apple orchard. He had never seen such a beautiful girl!

Hades stood in his disguise at the edge of the orchard and watched Persephone as she swung on the branches of the trees.

Finally, Persephone saw Hades standing nearby. In his tattered cloak, he looked like a poor and hungry traveler. Persephone was always generous, so she picked several apples from the tree and climbed down to meet him. "Please," said Persephone, "take these apples. They will give you strength for your journey."

Hades thanked Persephone for the apples and went on his way. "I must bring her to the Underworld!" he thought to himself. "It could never be a gloomy place with such a kind and beautiful queen as this!" Then Hades returned to the Underworld.

The next morning, Persephone decided to pick some apples for her mother. She ran to her favorite orchard and began picking the ripest apples she could find.

Suddenly there was a great rumble, and the ground split open before her! Out from below the earth charged two fierce, black horses pulling a dark chariot behind them. On the chariot rode Hades, wearing the black armor of the Underworld.

Persephone tried to run away, but Hades was too quick for her. He caught her and took her away with him in his chariot to the Underworld. The ground closed back up behind them. Not a trace of Persephone was to be seen except a few of the apples she left behind.

When Demeter came home from the fields, Persephone was nowhere to be seen. Demeter went to the orchard where Persephone had been picking apples, and found some apples spilled on the ground. "Something terrible has happened to Persephone!" cried Demeter. She ran to search for her daughter.

After looking everywhere for her daughter, Demeter decided to visit Helios, the god of the sun. "Helios sees everything on earth. He will help me find Persephone," she said.

"I have seen Persephone," Helios said. He told Demeter that Hades had taken Persephone to the Underworld to be his queen.

Demeter knew how unhappy Persephone would be in the Underworld. Demeter became sad and lonely for her daughter. The earth became cold and snowy, and the crops in the field faded and died.

In the Underworld, Persephone was sad and lonely, too. She tried to make her new home a more beautiful place, but nothing helped. The ground was too cold to plant seeds, and there was no sunshine to help them grow. Finally she asked Hades to let her return to the earth.

"But you are the queen of the Underworld!" exclaimed Hades. "Not many girls have the chance to be a queen. I am sure you will be happy here if you only stay a while longer."

Persephone became friends with Cerberus. Although he looked ferocious, he was lonely just like her. Sometimes he walked with her through the gloomy caves of the Underworld.

But even with her new friend, Persephone missed the sunny days and lush fields where she had played on the earth.

Demeter missed her daughter more and more each passing day. Finally she traveled to Mount Olympus, the home of the gods. She asked Zeus, the most powerful god of all, for his help.

"Hades has kidnapped my daughter Persephone and taken her to the Underworld to be his queen! Please help me bring her back to earth again!" begged Demeter.

Zeus saw that the earth had become cold and barren. He knew that he had to help Demeter to make the earth fruitful again. "I will ask Hades to return Persephone," said Zeus sternly. "But if she has eaten any food in the Underworld, I may not be able to help her. Anyone who eats the food of the dead belongs forever to Hades." With that, Zeus took his lightning bolt in hand and traveled to the Underworld.

"Hades!" thundered Zeus when he reached the gates of the Underworld. He made his way inside easily, for even fierce Cerberus was afraid of the king of the gods.

Zeus found Hades sitting sadly on his dark throne, watching Persephone. Persephone hardly looked like the beautiful girl she had been before. Her golden hair had grown dull, and her rosy cheeks were pale.

"Hades, I demand that you return Persephone to the earth. Demeter misses her terribly, and the earth has grown fruitless and barren since you stole her daughter away," said Zeus.

"Very well," sighed Hades. "I thought her beauty would make my Underworld a happier place, but she is only sad and silent since she has come. You may take her back to the earth."

But Hades was very clever. He did not want to lose his queen, so he decided to trick Zeus. When Zeus was getting ready to take Persephone back to earth, Hades took her aside for a moment. He told her she would need food for her journey. He offered her a pomegranate, a fruit which has juicy seeds to eat. Persephone ate just six pomegranate seeds before she returned to earth. But the pomegranate came from the Underworld. Persephone did not know that Hades had tricked her into eating the food of the dead.

Zeus carried Persephone back to the earth. When Persephone returned, Demeter was overjoyed. She was so happy to see her daughter that the earth bloomed again.

Suddenly, Hades appeared before them. "Wait!" he exclaimed. "Persephone has eaten the food of the dead! She ate six seeds from a pomegranate before she came back to earth. She must live in the Underworld forever!"

Zeus was angry about the trick Hades had played. He thought very carefully before he said, "You did eat six pomegranate seeds. For each seed, you will spend one month of the year in the Underworld. The other six months you will spend on earth."

And so each year when Persephone goes to the Underworld, winter comes to the earth. But when Persephone returns, her mother is overjoyed and summer reigns on earth.

Love

Persephone was a kind and gentle person who tried to find good in everyone. When Hades captured her and took her down to the Underworld, her mother's love for her was so strong that it affected the seasons on the earth. Although Persephone tried to find good in being in the Underworld, she missed her mother and her life on the earth too much. Demeter's love for Persephone was so powerful that she asked the king of the gods to help get her daughter back.

When you love someone very much, you will do anything for that person. Do you feel like that about someone? How do you show them that you love them?

George Washington and the Cherry Tree

A Tale of Honesty

Adapted by Catherine McCafferty
Illustrated by Jerry Harston

Many stories and books have been written about George Washington. When the American colonies fought for their freedom, George Washington led the soldiers against the British. When the brand-new country needed a leader, Washington served as its first president.

The legend of George Washington's honesty is just as famous as these true stories of bravery. It is called a legend because no one has any records to say that the story really happened. Did young George Washington chop down a cherry tree? Maybe not. But this legend shows just how important it is for everyone to tell the truth.

Let's go back now to the time when George Washington was a young boy. He had just received a gift from his father that was, to him, the best present a boy could ask for.

What a fine day it was for young George Washington! At just six years old, he had his very own hatchet. George was proud of his new hatchet. It felt solid in his small hands. Its blade was shiny and sharp. George swung the hatchet through the air just to see the sun shine on it.

His father stopped him. "A hatchet is not a toy, George," his father warned. "It can do much harm if you are not careful. Always be careful when you use it."

George nodded at his father's words. His father was talking to him like a man. Owning a hatchet was a serious thing, indeed. George promised he would always be very careful with it.

Once he was outside, though, George felt more excited than serious. His family's farm seemed full of things to cut. George started testing the hatchet's sharpness in the fields.

First George tested his hatchet on a row of weeds at the edge of the cornfield. It sliced through their thin stems. The row of tall weeds became a pile of cut weeds. George smiled. He took aim at the thicker stalks of the corn plants.

Whack! Three cornstalks fell with a rustle and a crunch. George stepped back, startled. He looked at his hatchet with a new respect. His father was right. He would have to be careful. Then George saw that an ear of corn had fallen to the ground. It was even thicker than the cornstalks. George's hatchet sliced the corncob in half with no problem.

Not far from the cornfield, George's father tended to his fruit trees. His father was proud of the sweet apples, peaches, and pears that the trees gave his family. He kept the trees' branches trimmed, and watched them for any sign of sickness.

Mr. Washington gave extra attention to his youngest tree. It was a cherry tree, and it had come from far away. The cherry tree had been just a sapling when Mr. Washington planted it. Each year, Mr. Washington watched it grow stronger. This year, there were blossoms on its branches. Perhaps, he thought, it might even give fruit. Mr. Washington thought of the fresh cherries they could pick. Then he thought of the cherry pies Mrs. Washington could bake with the sweet cherries. He smiled to himself as he gave the cherry tree a pat.

George ran up to Mr. Washington as he walked back to the house for supper. "This hatchet works well, Father," he said.

His father smiled. "Yes, I've seen you using it."

"Thank you again, Father, for such a wonderful gift," said George as he ran inside to get ready for dinner.

When they sat down for dinner, George laid his hatchet down in a corner of the room. All through dinner, he looked over at it. What could he do with it next?

George's mother noticed how George watched the hatchet. "I think it's time you put that hatchet to good use, George," she said. "Tomorrow, I would like you to chop kindling for the fire."

"Oh yes, Mother!" George said. "I can start tonight!"

Mrs. Washington said, "You need a good night's sleep first."

George put his hatchet under his bed. He climbed into bed and closed his eyes. George had a hard time falling asleep. He couldn't wait until morning. He saw himself chopping piles, and then mounds, and then mountains of kindling! When George finally fell asleep, he dreamed that he was a great woodcutter. With one sweep of his hatchet, he cut down whole forests.

The next morning, George hurried through his breakfast. As soon as he finished his last bite, he told his mother, "I'm ready to chop kindling now." His mother sent him out to the woodshed.

George looked around for the kindling. It was not a mountain of kindling. And it was barely a mound. Still, George went to work. He chopped the long, thin branches into small sticks. Then George chopped the small sticks into smaller sticks. Then he chopped the smaller sticks into pieces. George saw that the pieces were too small to be chopped further. He ran inside to tell his mother that he had finished his job.

"I'm finished, Mother. Is there any more kindling for me to chop?" George asked.

"No, George. You may play for a while," she said.

George didn't want to play. He wanted to chop more wood.

George wandered outside. George decided to test his hatchet again. He went to an old, thick fence post. On the first strike, his hatchet's blade sunk deep into the wood. George had to tug to pull it free. "Well, that was too thick," George thought. Then he saw the trunk of the young cherry tree.

The tree trunk looked just right. It wasn't full-grown as the apple and pear trees were. George chopped at the cherry tree. The blade dug into the tree trunk, but pulled free easily. Why, it would take just a few strokes of his hatchet to cut the tree down! George chopped until the tree fell. George looked proudly at the fallen tree. Then he remembered how much his father liked the cherry tree. And he remembered how his father had told him to be careful with the hatchet.

George hurried back to the woodshed and sat in a dark corner.

Mr. Washington saw the fallen tree on his way to the house. He saw that its trunk was cut through with many strokes. Then he realized there would be no cherries. There would be no cherry pies. After all his hard work and care, there would be no cherry tree. George's father sadly walked back to the house.

George saw his father walk past the woodshed. Slowly, he followed his father into the house. He held his hatchet tightly.

His father turned as he heard George come in the door. He looked at George. He looked at George's hatchet. George could see that his father was very angry. "George," he said, "do you know who cut down my cherry tree?"

George took a deep breath. He tried not to think about being punished. Instead George said, "I cannot tell a lie, Father. I cut down your cherry tree."

George looked at his feet. He felt like crying. "I wasn't careful with the hatchet. I'm sorry, Father." Then he held his breath and waited to hear what his punishment would be.

George felt his father's hands on his shoulders. "Look at me, Son," said Mr. Washington. George made himself look up at his father. To George's surprise, his father no longer seemed angry. In fact, Mr. Washington looked rather calm.

"You have been honest, Son," said Mr. Washington. "That means more to me than any cherry tree ever could."

Of course, George's father was disappointed that there would be no cherries to make cherry pies, but he was proud of his son for telling the truth. "So remember, you must always tell the truth," George's father added.

George never forgot those words. They were a lesson for life.

Honesty

Young George Washington was proud to have gotten a hatchet from his parents. Yet George was not careful with it and cut down his father's cherry tree. When he realized what he had done, George did not try to hide the mistake from his father. George knew that the right thing to do was to tell the truth, though his father could punish him. His father forgave him and even praised him for being honest.

Sometimes telling the truth seems scary. Did you ever tell the truth knowing that you might be punished? Being honest when you know someone may be hurt or upset is hard. Even if you are afraid, telling the truth is always better.

Thumbelina

A Tale of Patience

Adapted by Megan Musgrave

Illustrated by Jane Maday

165

There was once a woman who lived in a tiny cottage which had the most beautiful garden in the world. She was very happy tending her garden, but over time she became sad. She had no children who could share her garden with her. She decided to ask the old witch in her village for her help.

When the woman explained that she wanted a child, the old witch thought for a moment. Then she pulled a tiny bag out of a fold in her cloak. "Plant these wildflower seeds and tend to them carefully every day. Soon you will have your wish," said the witch.

The woman was overjoyed that the witch gave her a solution to her problem. She took the seeds home with her. The next day, she planted them in a sunny corner of her garden. It was the prettiest spot she could find. She watered and watched over the seeds every day.

Soon tiny green sprouts began to poke up out of the ground. Before long, the sprouts grew and blossomed into a beautiful patch of wildflowers.

In the center of the wildflower patch grew a single, beautiful tulip. Its deep pink petals were closed up tightly. The flower was so lovely that the woman could not resist bending down to smell it. As she knelt in front of the flower, its petals suddenly opened. The woman was amazed to find a tiny girl sitting inside. She wore a tulip petal for a dress and had long, gleaming hair.

"You are the most beautiful child I have ever seen! And you are hardly even as big as my thumb. Would you like to stay with me in my garden?" asked the woman.

"Oh, yes!" replied the tiny girl.

"I will call you Thumbelina," said the woman.

At home, she made Thumbelina a tiny bed out of an acorn shell. Thumbelina slept soundly under her rose petal blanket.

Thumbelina and her mother lived very happily in the garden the whole summer long. Thumbelina loved to play in the little pond in the middle of the garden, so her mother made her a tiny boat out of a maple leaf. Thumbelina rowed around the pond, using two blades of grass as oars. Her mother sat by the side of the pond and read stories to her while she played.

Sometimes, Thumbelina sang as she rowed. She had the most beautiful, silvery voice that her mother always loved to hear.

One day, a frog was hopping by the garden pond. He heard Thumbelina's beautiful voice. When he saw the tiny girl rowing her maple leaf boat he said, "What a lovely creature! I must take her away to my lily pad to be my wife."

The frog watched and waited until Thumbelina's mother went inside the cottage to get a cup of lemonade for Thumbelina. Then the frog jumped out from behind the reeds where he had been hiding and captured Thumbelina. He carried her away to the river where he lived and placed her on a lily pad. "Rest here while I go and make the plans for our wedding," said the frog. With that, he hopped away.

Thumbelina did not want to be the wife of a frog. She wanted to be back home with her mother. She became so sad that she began to cry. Her tiny tears fell into the river and made ripples in its glassy surface.

When the fish in the river saw Thumbelina crying, they decided to help her. They nibbled through the stem of her lily pad until it broke free and floated down the river, far away from the frog.

Thumbelina flowed gently on the river until finally the lily pad came to rest on a grassy bank.

Thumbelina climbed up the bank and found herself on the edge of a meadow. "I miss my home, but this will be a fine place to live until I can find my way back to Mother again," she said.

She wove herself a tiny hammock out of grass blades and hung it up beneath a large daisy which sheltered her from the dew at night. During the day she wandered through the meadow. If she was thirsty, she drank the dew off a blade of grass. If she was hungry, she had a bite of clover or some honeysuckle. She became friends with the butterflies and ladybugs in the meadow, and at night she slept safely under her daisy roof.

One day, Thumbelina noticed that the days were getting chilly. Fall was coming. Leaves began to fall from the trees.

The nights were becoming colder, too. She made herself a blanket out of cotton from the meadow, but soon it was not enough. "I am so cold and I don't know when I'll get back home! How will I keep warm in the winter?" cried Thumbelina. She began to take long walks, looking for a place where she could be safe and warm. One day, she found a small burrow inside a tree. She poked her head inside to see if anyone lived there.

Inside the little burrow lived a friendly old field mouse. The burrow was snug and cozy, for the mouse had lined it with cotton and hay from the meadow. "Excuse me," said Thumbelina quietly, "may I come into your warm burrow for a moment?"

The old field mouse almost never had any visitors in autumn, and was happy to have one. "Come in, come in! You poor dear. Come over by the fire and have a cup of tea."

Thumbelina told the field mouse of the horrible frog who took her away from her home. She told her how much she couldn't wait to get back to her mother and her garden.

The field mouse invited Thumbelina to stay with her for the winter. Together they gathered nuts, grains, and berries for the cold months ahead. Thumbelina sang songs and told stories, while the field mouse cooked their dinner or sewed by the fire.

One day it began to snow lightly. Thumbelina had never seen snow before, so she opened the door to peek outside. But as she looked outside, she saw something strange. Lying near the field mouse's front door was a young sparrow with a broken wing. He was shivering and he looked sad.

Thumbelina called the field mouse. Together they helped the sparrow into the burrow and fed him some soup.

Thumbelina, the sparrow, and the old field mouse passed the winter together in the burrow. Thumbelina helped to mend the sparrow's wing so that he would be able to fly again. She told them stories of her kind mother and the beautiful garden where she was born. She hoped she would see her home again.

One day, Thumbelina poked her head outside the burrow again. Tiny green shoots were beginning to appear all over the meadow. "Spring is coming!" she shouted to her friends.

Soon the days were warm and sunny. The sparrow decided it was time to leave the burrow. "Thumbelina," he said, "you saved my life. Now I would like to help you find your mother."

Thumbelina said good-bye to her field mouse friend and climbed on top of the sparrow. She held on tight to the sparrow's feathers as he flew high above the trees.

"Do you think we will ever find my mother?" Thumbelina asked the sparrow.

"Yes, but first I have something special to show you," said the sparrow. He flew deep into the forest and landed gently in a thicket. All around them, beautiful flowers blossomed. No sooner had they landed, than a lily opened and out stepped a tiny boy. He wore a crown on his head, and he had a pair of shiny wings.

"I am the Prince of the Flowers," said the boy. "Live with us and be the Princess of the Flowers." He gave her a tiny pair of silvery wings and a beautiful crown of gold.

But Thumbelina missed her mother. She agreed to come back to the prince, but she had to see her mother. When Thumbelina flew into her mother's garden, the woman was so overjoyed to see her tiny daughter again that she laughed and cried for joy.

Patience

Away from home, Thumbelina was alone and very scared. But she never gave up hope of returning to her mother and her beautiful garden. Thumbelina was patient and kind to every creature she met. She knew that one day someone would be able to help her return to her home.

Sometimes patience is all you have to get you through a situation. Did you ever want something very badly when you knew you had to wait to get it? It seems like you had to wait forever! Still, if you are patient, the waiting doesn't seem so bad and the reward, in the end, is great.

A Brer Rabbit Story

A Tale of Ingenuity

Adapted by Megan Musgrave
Illustrated by Rusty Fletcher

I am going to tell you a story about Brer Rabbit and Brer Fox. But first, you ought to know a thing or two about rabbits and foxes. Rabbits and foxes just never seem to get along. This is probably because foxes are always trying to make a meal out of rabbits, and rabbits are always trying to outfox foxes.

Brer Rabbit was the craftiest rabbit ever to cross a fox's path. Brer Fox was always trying to catch Brer Rabbit, but Brer Rabbit always had a trick up his sleeve. One day, Brer Fox decided to get Brer Rabbit once and for all.

Brer Fox knew that Brer Rabbit liked to go over to the farmer's garden every day for carrots and cabbages. Brer Fox decided to hide behind a big tree on the road to the garden and wait for Brer Rabbit to pass. The tree was on the edge of a briar patch, full of bushes with thorns and burrs.

"I'm a-gonna wait right here for that sneaky rabbit an' cook 'im up in a rabbit stew!" said Brer Fox, proud of his sneaky plan.

Soon Brer Rabbit came hippity-hopping down the road to the garden. Brer Fox jumped out from behind the tree and grabbed him up as quick as he could.

"I'm a-gonna brew a stew out of you, Rabbit!" said Brer Fox.

Brer Rabbit had to do some fast talking. "You can cook me up in a big ol' pot an' serve me for dinner, but please don't throw me into dat briar patch yonder!" cried Brer Rabbit.

Brer Fox thought for a moment. "Now, maybe dat stew would be too much bother for me. I'm a-gonna roast you up instead!"

"You can fire up your ol' stove an' roast me an' serve me up with fried taters, but pleeease don't throw me in dat briar patch!" pleaded Brer Rabbit.

This was starting to sound like a lot of work to Brer Fox. He really just wanted to get that rabbit out of his hair once and for all. "Naw, your scrawny hide ain't worth troublin' over. I'm jus' gonna string you up from that ol' hick'ry tree an' git you outta my hair," said Brer Fox.

"String me up an' let me swing, but whatever you do, please don't throw me into that terr'ble briar patch!" cried Brer Rabbit.

Suddenly, Brer Fox knew just the thing to do. "Seems to me jus' about the worst thing I kin do is throw you into dat ol' briar patch, Rabbit," said Brer Fox. "An' dat's jus' what I'm a-gonna do!" And with that, Brer Fox swung Brer Rabbit over his head and threw him into the middle of the briar patch.

"Yow! Oh, I'm a-gonna die!" yowled Brer Rabbit as he sailed through the air.

But as soon as he landed in the briar patch, all Brer Fox could hear was Brer Rabbit hee-hawing and guffawing in gigglement. Brer Fox knew he'd been had again.

"Oh, Mister Fox, you shoulda known better! Y'see, I was born in dis here briar patch! I'm as happy as a crawfish in a river bed!"

Brer Fox was hoppin' mad. "I got to git dat rabbit good, once an' for all. He's a-goin' to Miss Goose's birthday party tomorrow, so I'm a-gonna make real friendly-like, an' go an' walk over to dat party with him. An' when we git to crossin' the river, I'm a-gonna throw dat rabbit in! He'll be gone for good, sure as shootin'!"

The next day, Brer Rabbit was at his house getting all spruced up for Miss Goose's party. When he saw Brer Fox come a-trottin' up his path, he wrapped himself up in a blanket and acted real sick-like.

"What's all this moanin' about, Rabbit?" asked Brer Fox.

"Oh, I'm sick as an ol' dawg, Mister Fox. I ain't a-gonna make it to Miss Goose's party after all," sighed Brer Rabbit.

"This is a-gonna help wit' my plan jus' fine," thought Brer Fox. He said to Brer Rabbit, "Now, you know you gonna be sorry if you miss dat party, Rabbit. I'm a-gonna carry you."

"You're mighty kind, Mister Fox. But surely I couldn't ride on your back without a saddle," said Brer Rabbit sneakily. Brer Fox went off to find a saddle. While he was gone, Brer Rabbit picked some flowers for Miss Goose and hid them under his blanket.

Brer Fox came back wearing a saddle. "Up you go," he said.

"You're mighty kind, Mister Fox, but surely I couldn't ride along in dis saddle without havin' a bridle to steer you along," said Brer Rabbit.

While Brer Fox went to fetch a bridle, Brer Rabbit rummaged around in his closet to find a brown paper bag. "I'm a-gonna give that fox a surprise he'll never forgit. He thinks he can outfox me, but I'm the foxiest rabbit this side of the Mississippi," Brer Rabbit said with chuckleness.

When Brer Fox returned, he was wearing a bridle as well as the saddle. He was all ready to go just like an old horse at the starting gate. "Rabbit," he said, "Miss Goose ain't a-gonna take it kindly if we're late for her party. You climb on up here now, an' let's git a-goin'." He chuckled to himself, thinking that soon he would be rid of that rabbit forever.

"You're terrible kind to an ol' sick rabbit like me, Mister Fox," said Brer Rabbit with a groan. He climbed into the saddle, and they were on their way.

Soon they came to the river. As Brer Fox stepped onto the bridge he thought, "I'm a-gonna throw that buggery rabbit off into kingdom come. Yep, this is just the spot."

But Brer Rabbit was ready for Brer Fox's sneaky trick. As soon as he felt Brer Fox stop over the middle of the river, he filled the paper bag with air. He said, "What you stoppin' for, Mister Fox?"

"I'm a-gonna throw you into kingdom come, Rabbit!"

"Oh, no you're not. Giddyup!" shouted Brer Rabbit. And with that, he popped that bag right over Brer Fox's ears.

"Yeeoow!" shrieked Brer Fox. He thought a hunter had taken a clean shot at him. He jumped up in the air like a mad grasshopper and took off down the other side of the bridge.

Brer Fox galloped toward Miss Goose's house with Brer Rabbit hanging on to the saddle and yodeling all the way.

"Giddyup, you ol' nag!" cried Brer Rabbit. Poor Brer Fox just kept on galloping along past the briar patch, past the farmer's garden, past the duck pond, and right up to Miss Goose's house. Miss Goose, Miss Sheep, and Miss Pig had heard Brer Rabbit yodeling from a long way off. When Brer Fox came galloping up with Brer Rabbit on his back, they thought they had never seen anything so funny.

"Whoa!" shouted Brer Rabbit as Brer Fox galloped up to Miss Goose's house. Brer Fox skidded to a stop and flopped on the ground right on the doorstep. "Aft'noon, ladies," said Brer Rabbit as he climbed down. "I am very sorry for bein' late, but my ol' horse here jus' don't run like he used to."

Miss Goose, Miss Sheep, and Miss Pig burst with gigglement. They thought Brer Rabbit sure got Brer Fox good this time.

Poor old Brer Fox sat in the front yard of Miss Goose's house, sputtering and gluttering and catching his breath. He was so mad he could spit. "That rabbit tricked me good dis time. I don' know how I'm a-gonna do it, but I'm a-gonna git dat rabbit one day, once an' for all," he fumed. Brer Fox felt a little bit better after tasting Miss Goose's birthday cake.

Ever since that day, ol' Brer Fox has kept trying to outsmart Brer Rabbit. And ever since that day sneaky Brer Rabbit has been just one step ahead of Brer Fox.

So if you ever see a rabbit hopping around in a briar patch, or if you glimpse a fox snooping around a farmer's garden, it just might be crafty ol' Brer Rabbit and sneaky ol' Brer Fox trying to outfox each other again.

Ingenuity

Brer Rabbit was much smaller than Brer Fox, but he used his wits to beat Brer Fox again and again. Brer Rabbit was clever enough to know that he could not win in a match of strength. He came up with ideas to outsmart Brer Fox, and, in turn, make Brer Fox do the exact opposite of what he was planning on doing.

Being clever is sometimes the best weapon against a bully. If someone bigger than you tries to scare you, think of how scared this bully would be if you turned the tables on them. Use your wits to defend yourself or to avoid a confrontation altogether. It will show who really is the bigger person.

Androcles and the Lion

A Tale of Friendship

Adapted by Sarah Toast

Illustrated by Yuri Salzman

In ancient Rome there lived a poor slave named Androcles. His cruel master made him work from daybreak until long past nightfall. Androcles had very little time to rest and very little to eat. One day, he decided to run away from his harsh master, even though he would be breaking the law.

In the dark of night, Androcles got up from the miserable heap of straw and rags that served as his bed. Crouching low so he was no taller than the bushes that dotted the fields, the young slave moved swiftly away from his master's land.

Clouds covered the moon that night, and Androcles crossed the open fields unseen. It was only when he came to the wild woods that Androcles dared to stand up tall again.

Androcles found a sheltered place at the foot of a tall tree. There he lay himself down and fell fast asleep.

When Androcles awoke, he hiked deeper into the woods so he wouldn't be found by his master. There he looked for water and something to eat. But other than a few berries, there was no food to be found.

Day after day, Androcles searched for food. And day after day, he went hungry. Androcles grew so weary and weak that at last he was afraid he wouldn't live through the night. He had just enough strength to creep up to the mouth of a cave that he had passed many times. Androcles crawled into the cave and fell into a deep sleep.

As Androcles lay sleeping, a lion was hunting in the woods nearby. The lion caught a small animal for his supper. He ate his meal beside a stream in the woods. Then he set off for his cave as the morning began to fill the sky with light.

Just before reaching the cave where Androcles slept, the lion stepped on the fallen branch of a thorn tree. A large thorn went deep into his paw.

The lion let out an angry roar, which woke Androcles with a terrible start. From the mouth of the cave, Androcles could see the lion rolling on the ground in pain. The lion's roars echoed loudly in the cave.

Androcles was terrified that the lion would attack him. But the lion held out his hurt paw to Androcles. Even from a distance, Androcles could see the large thorn in the lion's paw.

Androcles found some courage and came closer. He slowly sat down on the ground near the beast. To Androcles' astonishment, the huge lion flopped his great paw into the young man's lap. He could tell that this beast was in great pain and needed help.

Androcles spoke soothing words to the lion as he carefully pulled the thorn from the lion's paw. "Don't worry, handsome lion. We'll have this thorn out in no time," he said softly. The lion seemed to understand that Androcles was helping him. When the thorn was gone, the lion rubbed his head against Androcles' shoulder and purred a rumbling purr.

Androcles was no longer afraid of the lion. The lion was very grateful to Androcles for pulling the thorn out of his paw, and didn't even mind that Androcles had moved into his cave. They became fast friends.

The lion slept most of the day. And at night, he hunted for food while Androcles slept. In the morning, the lion would bring fresh meat to Androcles, who would build a little fire to cook his newly caught meal.

Every morning after Androcles ate, he and the lion played for a while in the woods nearby. The lion showed Androcles how much he liked him by rubbing his head against the man and licking his hands and feet. Androcles scratched the lion behind the ears and petted his sleek back.

One morning, as Androcles was cooking what the lion had brought him, four soldiers suddenly appeared and surprised him.

"We saw the smoke from your fire," they said. "We have come to arrest you for running away from your master."

Androcles did not know what to do. He tried to run from the soldiers, but they were too fast for him. Two soldiers sprinted after Androcles. When they caught him, they tied his hands behind his back.

Androcles cried out as the soldiers tried to carry him off.

The lion awoke with a start. Before he could get to his feet to help Androcles, the other two soldiers threw a strong rope net over him. They attached the ends of the net to two stout poles and carried the angry lion out of the woods.

Androcles was forced to march to a huge arena in Rome.

One soldier said to Androcles, "Your punishment is to fight a hungry lion!"

It was the custom in Rome at that time to entertain the people with battles fought on the sandy floor of the arena, which was circled by rows and rows of seats.

The soldiers took Androcles to a prison under the arena seats. Then they left him alone in his prison cell. Androcles had never felt so scared or so alone. It was a long time before the soldiers came back for Androcles.

Suddenly, Androcles heard a trumpet blast. Then the bars to Androcles' prison were opened. A soldier took Androcles and pushed him onto the field.

Androcles found himself alone in the middle of the huge arena. Hundreds of people were watching him, waiting for the battle to begin. Androcles noticed a large cage at the end of the field. When a lion's roar sounded throughout the arena, the people grew excited.

The trumpet sounded a second time, and the bars to the lion's cage were opened. In a moment, a lean lion bounded out of the cell, roaring with hunger. The people sitting in the arena shouted, "Hooray!" The crowd sounded like a mighty roar to Androcles.

The lion crouched only for a moment, but in that moment Androcles recognized his friend from the forest.

The lion let out another thundery roar and bounded across the arena in three long leaps. He stopped right in front of Androcles and gently lifted his big paw.

Androcles gave a mighty shout of joy. "Lion, you remember me!" he cried. He took the lion's paw in his hand and patted it lovingly. Then the lion rubbed his great head against the young man's shoulder. Androcles scratched the lion behind the ears, just as he had done at home in their forest cave.

The crowd of people in the arena was stunned into silence. They had never seen anything like this in the arena before. As the crowd sat in silence, Androcles and his best friend began to frolic and play. Everyone turned to each other and started talking at once. They wanted to know what this boy's secret was for taming the ferocious lion.

The Emperor, who watched every game in the arena, motioned for the crowd to be quiet. Then he called Androcles to approach him and his royal subjects.

"How did you tame this vicious lion?" the Emperor asked Androcles.

"I merely helped him when he needed help, Your Highness," Androcles replied. "That is why he spared my life."

The Emperor could see that Androcles and the lion were true friends. The Emperor freed Androcles and the lion. The lion returned to the cave in the wild woods, and Androcles became a free man in Rome.

Androcles often went for a walk in the woods to visit his good friend. As soon as they saw each other, they played and frolicked as if they had never been apart.

Androcles and the Lion

Friendship

Androcles and the lion make an unlikely pair, but their friendship proved to be strong and true. When Androcles removed the thorn from the lion's paw, a friendship based on trust and compassion was born. It was this strong bond that kept the lion from attacking Androcles in the arena.

Friendships are best when they are based on trust. Friends should be caring and thoughtful to one another. Do you have a best friend? What do you like best about your friend? What do you think he or she likes best about you?

The Brownie of Blednock

A Tale of Generosity

Adapted by Jennifer Boudart
Illustrated by Gwen Connelly

Nighttime was falling over the town of Blednock. The people who lived there were doing what they did every ordinary day. Women stood on their doorsteps talking about the harvest. Children played in the town square. No one knew it, but something special was about to happen. It all began with a humming noise. The people of Blednock lined up along Main Street and looked down the road.

The humming kept getting louder. It was like the way you would hum to yourself if you were happy.

They could see that somebody was coming down the road. People began to whisper to each other. Who was this visitor to Blednock? Visitors came from near and far, but no one had seen a person who looked like this before. And what was with the strange humming sound?

The stranger was as small as a boy, but he had a long, brown beard. He wore a long, pointed hat and tiny, curled-up shoes. He walked closer and closer, and the humming got louder and louder.

"Do you think he speaks our language?" whispered one man.

"Has he come to town to buy or sell?" wondered another.

Soon the crowd was quiet. That's when they heard what the stranger was humming: "Any work for Aiken-Drum? Any work for Aiken-Drum?"

What was Aiken-Drum? No one seemed to know. The people were more curious than ever. They gathered around the strange visitor, who kept right on humming.

Then Granny, the wisest woman in the town, had something to say. "I think Aiken-Drum is what our visitor calls himself," she announced. "I believe he is a brownie."

Granny hopped onto a stump and shook the brownie's hand. "Speak up, Brownie," said Granny. So he did.

"The ways of brownies are very different from the ways of people," explained Aiken-Drum. "In our land, we learn to do good by serving others."

The little brownie explained that he was from somewhere far away, and there was not enough work in his land. "I don't need money, clothes, or fancy living," said the brownie. "I just need a dry place to sleep and something warm to drink at bedtime." In return, Aiken-Drum promised to do any kind of work.

"I've heard brownies are the best workers," Granny told her neighbors. "If there's a town that needs a helping hand, it's Blednock," she added. Granny was right. The new church needed building. The bridge needed mending.

That is how a brownie came to live in the town of Blednock. Granny was the unofficial president of the brownie welcoming committee. All the townspeople chipped in to try and make the new visitor comfortable in his new home.

The blacksmith let Aiken-Drum sleep in a dry corner of his barn. He gave the brownie just a simple horse's blanket to keep warm at night, for that is what Aiken-Drum requested.

"We brownies don't need anything fancy. A simple blanket from the stable will do," reminded Aiken-Drum.

The blacksmith knew enough not to force any extra special treatment or fancy pillows on the brownie. The blacksmith knew that keeping his sleeping area simple was a way to show respect for Aiken-Drum's wishes. He wouldn't want to upset the little man who had come so far just to be helpful.

At the end of each day, Granny brought the brownie something warm to drink. She too remembered Aiken-Drum's simple needs.

The rest of the townspeople tried to spot Aiken-Drum working whenever they could. But it always seemed that he was hurrying to one place or another. No one really saw him do any work. In fact, Aiken-Drum seemed to do all his work at night!

Every morning, the blacksmith found only an empty mug in the barn and the horse blanket folded neatly in the corner.

Soon, all of the people of Blednock were sharing stories about the magical work of the little brownie.

"Aiken-Drum fixed a broken wheel on my wagon last night. He must have known that I was going to take my grain to the miller today," chuckled Baker Smith. "I will be forever grateful to that curious little brownie."

Old Mother Jones also had a story about the brownie. "While I was asleep with fever, Aiken-Drum came. He cleaned my whole house and cooked a big batch of soup!" she said.

"Aiken-Drum brought all my sheep to safety. He took them into the barn just before last night's storm!" said Farmer Adams. "It's too bad those sheep can't talk, but I know that it was the brownie who led my sheep into the barn. And he did it so quietly, too. I didn't hear a thing until the storm kicked in."

More and more stories were being told of the good work that Aiken-Drum had been doing around Blednock. Wherever work needed to be done, Aiken-Drum was there. No one even had to ask. And the town was looking better than it ever had. The new church that the brownie built was even prettier than anyone had hoped for. The town was delighted!

Aiken-Drum did take breaks from time to time. On still evenings, when fireflies began to wink, the brownie sat by the river. He was never alone for long. The children of Blednock came to join him.

Children loved Aiken-Drum. He loved them, too. They crowded around, giggling and asking to play this game or that one:

"Tell us a story, Aiken-Drum."

"Teach us a song, Aiken-Drum."

"Show us a dance, Aiken-Drum."

"Play hide-and-seek, Aiken-Drum."

Aiken-Drum would start a bonfire and tell stories and play with the children until their parents called them for dinner. When the children went off to their houses, Aiken-Drum went off to work. That's the way he liked it.

Everyone thought things around Blednock were better than ever thanks to Aiken-Drum. Well, almost everyone. Miss Daisy Fain thought differently. "I think things are unfair around Blednock," she said to whoever was near. "It is not right to make a brownie work so hard for so little."

Miss Daisy's neighbors shook their heads at her. "Aiken-Drum made it plain, Miss Daisy," they would say with a sigh. "Brownies work only for the love of making people happy. Brownies do not need to be paid."

Miss Daisy just sniffed. She was sure he needed something more. He simply was too shy to ask. Why, who wouldn't want more than the corner of a stable and a horse blanket?

Finally, Miss Daisy decided to do what she knew was best. Everyone would thank her for it later, Aiken-Drum most of all.

One night, Miss Daisy tiptoed into the blacksmith's barn. The brownie was not there. Miss Daisy placed a pair of her husband's pants next to his mug. They would be too big for Aiken-Drum. Still, he would love them.

Well, you can guess what happened. Aiken-Drum took one look at those pants and knew what was happening. Someone had tried to pay him! His new friends had forgotten what mattered most to a brownie, so he disappeared that very night. No one saw him go.

The townspeople were very angry at Miss Daisy. She not only tried to pay a brownie, but she paid him with smelly, old pants!

After that, the people often spoke of Aiken-Drum with broken hearts and heavy sighs. The children were saddest of all. Still, once in a while, when the wind was just right, they could hear the sound of humming floating across the river.

Generosity

Generosity is when someone does a deed simply from the goodness of his or her own heart. A generous person does not expect a reward for his or her good deed. The brownie was generous with all the work he did for the people of Blednock. He did not want money for his work. He didn't need praise or a fancy home. He worked simply for the sake of helping people in need.

Whom would you consider a generous person? How have they shown their generosity? In what ways can you show that you are generous?

Icarus and Daedalus

A Tale of Obedience

Adapted by Sarah Toast

Illustrated by John Hanley

Long ago in ancient Greece there lived a very clever man named Daedalus. He was a great inventor and a skillful engineer and architect. Daedalus planned magnificent buildings that even had running water in the bathrooms. He was very proud of his skill.

Daedalus left Athens, the city of his birth, and went to the island of Crete in the blue Aegean Sea. He took with him his young son, Icarus.

King Minos of Crete commanded Daedalus to build a labyrinth, or maze, to imprison a fearful monster called the Minotaur. The Minotaur is a monster that is half-man and half-bull. Daedalus built the huge labyrinth underneath the king's stone palace. The labyrinth had so many false turns and dead-ends that no one who entered it could ever find a way out.

When the labyrinth was finished, the angry Minotaur was sealed inside it. When the Minotaur roared, the palace shook. The king was satisfied that the monster was safely locked away.

Daedalus had been on Crete for a long time. He wanted to return home. So he went to King Minos and said, "Great King, with your permission, I shall take my leave. My work is done, and I wish to return to Athens with my son."

"You will do no such thing," said King Minos. "You know the secret of the labyrinth. How do I know you won't tell somebody how to find the way through the twisting passageways?"

"I pledge that I will do no such thing!" protested Daedalus.

But the king ordered his guards to seize Daedalus and Icarus. The father and son were locked in a tall tower at the very edge of the palace grounds.

Despite all of the good Daedalus had done for the king, Daedalus and Icarus were kept under close guard in the prison tower. It would have done them no good to escape the tower, because King Minos also ruled the surrounding seas. The king's soldiers inspected every ship that left the shores of Crete. And if they were caught escaping, they would be sent to the labyrinth.

"Father, are we going to be locked in this tower forever?" asked Icarus.

"I am a great inventor, Icarus," replied Daedalus. "This certainly is a difficult problem, but I shall think of a solution."

After days of being locked in the tower, Daedalus and Icarus needed fresh air. Daedalus climbed the stairway and led Icarus to the rooftop of the tower. Its great height made Daedalus fearful for Icarus' safety.

From the rooftop, Daedalus and Icarus watched the gulls and eagles soaring and gliding through the air. The birds flew very close to the tower. Daedalus studied with fascination the birds' wings as they flew.

"Icarus, my son, I have an idea," said Daedalus. "King Minos may rule the land and the sea, but he does not rule the air!"

"What do you mean?" asked Icarus. "Only birds can fly through the air."

"That is because they have wings!" said Daedalus. "I want you to help me catch some birds. We need many feathers of all sizes."

Daedalus watched closely the way birds use their wings to take off and fly. He studied the way feathers fit together to cover the birds' wings. He noted the weight and the size of the wings in proportion to their bodies.

Icarus watched his father intently as he laid out a row of long feathers. Then his father laid a row of smaller feathers below that. He sewed them together with linen thread and a needle that he carried in his pouch.

Daedalus laid down many more rows of feathers which Icarus held in place for him. Finally, Daedalus softened some beeswax and fastened the rows of feathers together with the wax.

At last Daedalus was finished. He held up a beautiful pair of wings! Daedalus tied the wings to his arms and shoulders with thin strips of leather. Cautiously, he fluttered the wings.

Daedalus then moved the wings up and down with strong beats. As the wings moved, he could feel himself lifting from the roof of the tower!

"Stop, Father! Make my wings now!" Icarus begged.

Daedalus took his wings off and made a smaller set of wings for his son. Again he used wax to fasten many of the feathers. Then he tied the wings to Icarus.

"Just watch me first," said Daedalus to his son. "I'll try out the wings. If they work well, we'll both practice flying together."

Daedalus spread his wings, flapped them once, and caught the wind. Out he soared from the tower, lifting and falling on the air currents like a bird.

Icarus thought his father looked like a god as he flew through the air. The boy couldn't wait any longer to fly himself.

Icarus stood on tiptoe at the edge of the tower, flapped his wings, and took off. He swooped and soared, like his father. As he flew, he shouted for joy. "I'm a bird! I'm a god!" he cried.

"Icarus! Go back!" shouted Daedalus. "Go back to the tower!"

Daedalus landed on the rooftop and called again to Icarus, "Come back!"

The boy circled around the tower twice and did a somersault in the air, before he came back to where his father stood.

"Son, we have much to learn about flying. And you have much to learn about obeying your father!" said Daedalus. "We will have to practice to become strong and skillful enough to fly all the way across the Aegean," Daedalus explained.

Daedalus and Icarus practiced flying every day. Their muscles became strong. When Daedalus judged that he and Icarus were ready to make the long trip over the sea, he sat Icarus down.

"Son, it is important that you heed my words. If you fly too low, too close to the waves," Daedalus explained, "your feathers will get wet. Then, your wings will be too heavy to fly."

"And if you fly too high," Daedalus went on, "the heat of the sun will melt the wax that holds your wings together."

"I understand, Father," said Icarus, but he was barely listening.

No sooner had his father finished telling Icarus not to fly too low or too high, than the boy ran to the very edge of the rooftop and leapt off. He flapped his outspread wings and headed for the sea with Daedalus close behind him.

When the two reached the blue Aegean, Daedalus shouted a reminder to his son. The father and son rode the rising currents of air like birds. They made long, slow turns, first one way and then the other in the brilliant blue sky. After flying contentedly side by side, Daedalus took the lead.

Icarus did a somersault in the air, then caught up to his father. Daedalus gestured for Icarus to stay at a safe middle level.

Icarus, however, wanted to fly higher, up to where the gods lived. While Daedalus flew on in front, unaware, Icarus beat his wings hard and rose up and up. The warmth of the sun felt good on his back, and Icarus rose still higher.

The same warm sun melted the wax on Icarus' wings. First only a few feathers and then many slipped off of the wings as the wax turned to liquid. Suddenly, Icarus dropped straight down, down into the cold sea.

When Daedalus looked back, he could no longer see his son. Alarmed, Daedalus flew about in circles looking for the boy. At last, Daedalus flew close enough to the water to see the feathers floating on the sea. He knew then that his son had drowned.

Daedalus wept as he flew alone. If only his son had listened to him, then they would be flying to freedom together.

Obedience

Icarus got carried away and did not obey his father Daedelus' warning about flying too close to the sun. Daedelus was a scientist and knew flying too close to the sun and the water would affect the wax on the wings. Icarus should have respected his father's warning.

Often children think that they don't need the advice that adults give them. Yet, adults were once children, too. They have made mistakes and learned from their experiences. Adults tell you what to do because they care and do not want you to get hurt doing things that they know can be dangerous.

The Wild Swans

A Tale of Perseverance

Adapted by Brian Conway

Illustrated by Kathy Mitchell

Once there was a king who had much happiness and great fortune. Of all his treasures, he was proudest of his four children, the most perfect children in the land. His three fine, strong sons would do anything for their father. And the king's greatest joy, his daughter Elise, was clearly the dearest, sweetest, and most beautiful child in all the world.

Elise spent much of her time in her garden. Next to her three brothers and her father, her lovely roses were Elise's greatest treasures. She would spend hour after hour caring for them.

Then one day the king hurried to find Elise. He was very worried. "I have terrible news," he told her. "You are in danger."

The king had many treasures, but he also had many wicked and powerful enemies. They were evil sorcerers and magicians who believed no one should have as much happiness as the king.

"I fear for your safety," the king told his daughter. "You must go away from me now."

"But, Father," Elise cried, "what about you and my brothers?"

The king sighed. "Your brothers have been taken away from us," he sadly told her. "I know not where. I cannot stand to lose you, too."

The king told the princess to go with his trusted servants, who would take her to safety in their home in the forest.

"When you're old enough," said the king, "find your brothers and come back to me."

He kissed her good-bye. Elise did as her father said. She lived hidden away in the servants' house for many years. She was treated well, but she was very unhappy. Elise longed to see her three beloved brothers and her father again.

When Elise was old enough, she set off to find her brothers. She had no idea where to look, but she knew in her heart they were still alive. She had a feeling inside that told her they needed her help.

After several days of wandering and hoping for some sign, Elise met an old woman picking berries in the forest.

"I am looking for my three brothers," Elise told the woman. "They are fine, strong princes. Have you seen them?"

"I have seen nothing all day but three white swans with golden crowns on their heads," the old woman said. "They were sunning themselves on the shore."

She directed Elise to the spot. There, Elise found three white feathers. She clutched them close to her and fell asleep while she waited for the swans to return.

Just before sunset, Elise woke up to see three majestic swans gliding down to the shore. They landed beside her, and, as the last ray of sunshine disappeared, the three swans changed into three princes. Elise was overjoyed to see her brothers again! They held her close and told her what had happened to them.

Many years ago, an evil sorcerer had come to the castle. This sorcerer vowed to ruin the king's happiness, which he did the moment he turned the three handsome princes into swans. Since that day, they have lived as swans during the day and humans during the night.

"We have looked for you," the eldest brother told Elise. "But you were very well hidden."

"We have seen our father," the second brother told Elise. "He is safe, but very unhappy. He now serves the sorcerer."

"He cannot help us," added the third brother. "But each day he wishes we will find each other and make things right again."

Elise promised to help free her brothers from the sorcerer's wicked spell. Her brothers told her of an enchanted land far across the sea where they might find a way to break the spell.

"Take me with you," Elise urged them. "I know I can help."

Her brothers prepared a net to carry their sister in. The next morning, they flew high above the sea, carrying Elise as she slept. They rushed to reach land by nightfall, or else all three brothers and their sister would drop into the sea and be lost forever.

After two days' flight, they arrived at the kingdom across the sea. It was said that the Fairy Queen Morgana lived there. Surely she would know how to help them. Elise's brothers found her a cave to rest in while they searched for Queen Morgana.

As Elise fell asleep, she wished for a way to free her brothers from the spell. Then Queen Morgana came to Elise in a dream.

"Only you can free your brothers," Queen Morgana whispered to Elise. "But you must sacrifice greatly."

"Oh, I will," Elise promised. Then she listened carefully.

"Take the things you treasure most," Queen Morgana said, "and craft a shirt for each brother. This may take a very long time, but when you cover the swans with them, the spell will be broken. There is one more thing," she added. "You may not speak until the shirts are made. If you do, your words will pierce your brothers' hearts like arrows."

With that Queen Morgana disappeared. Elise awoke to find the cave surrounded with hundreds of lovely rosebushes, like the ones she'd had as a child. She knew what she had to do.

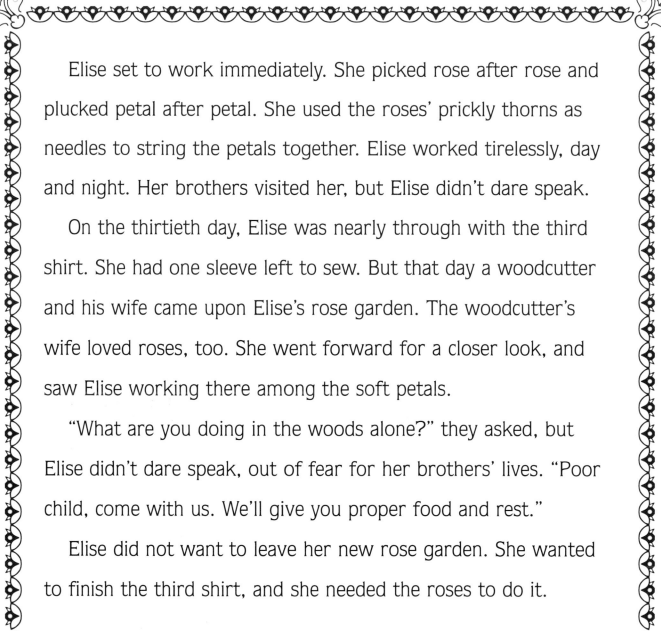

Elise set to work immediately. She picked rose after rose and plucked petal after petal. She used the roses' prickly thorns as needles to string the petals together. Elise worked tirelessly, day and night. Her brothers visited her, but Elise didn't dare speak.

On the thirtieth day, Elise was nearly through with the third shirt. She had one sleeve left to sew. But that day a woodcutter and his wife came upon Elise's rose garden. The woodcutter's wife loved roses, too. She went forward for a closer look, and saw Elise working there among the soft petals.

"What are you doing in the woods alone?" they asked, but Elise didn't dare speak, out of fear for her brothers' lives. "Poor child, come with us. We'll give you proper food and rest."

Elise did not want to leave her new rose garden. She wanted to finish the third shirt, and she needed the roses to do it.

Elise gathered up the shirts and as many roses as she could carry. Then she went sadly with the woodcutter and his wife.

Elise stayed there for many days and did as the woodcutter and his wife asked. At night, though, she would stay awake to sew the last shirt. Before long, Elise ran out of rose petals.

Elise crept out of the house that night and plucked the petals from the woodcutter's wife's prized roses. At sunrise, she had one cuff left to sew as the woodcutter's wife came to see her.

"Ungrateful girl!" she shouted. "You've ruined my roses!"

Flying the skies in search of some sign of their sister, Elise's brothers heard the shouts of the woodcutter's wife. They flew to the house. They squawked at the woodcutter, who ran in fear for his bow. Elise quickly spread the three shirts over the swans.

Before her eyes, the swans became men again!

Elise ran to her brothers' arms. The youngest brother, who wore the unfinished shirt, still had some feathers on one arm, but he did not mind.

Elise, anxious to speak now that the spell had been broken, explained everything to the woodcutter and his wife. "I'm sorry that I have been so difficult, when you have been so kind," said Elise. "My brothers and I thank you. We will repay you."

Elise and her brothers took all the rosebushes from the forest cave and planted them in the garden behind the woodcutter's house. Then they sent for their father the very next day. The king now had the strength and desire to escape the evil sorcerer. He journeyed by ship to the family's new home.

Elise and her three brothers prepared a new castle for their father, who became the king of a new land.

Perseverance

Perseverance is when you strive for something and don't give up, even when it seems like the odds are against you. Elise worked day and night, without speaking, to break the spell cast on her brothers. No matter how hard her task seemed, Elise knew she could not stop and she could not speak, or her brothers would suffer. Nothing was more important to Elise than saving her brothers.

When a task is important to you, it is worth all your effort. Imagine if a member of your family were in trouble, and you were the only one who could help. Wouldn't you do everything possible to help, even if it were very difficult?

Ali Baba

A Tale of Loyalty

Adapted by Brian Conway
Illustrated by Anthony Lewis

In a town in Persia there lived a man called Ali Baba. He was a poor woodcutter, and he struggled each day to feed his wife and children. All he ever wanted was to own a shop in the town, sell goods to his neighbors, and have plenty for his family.

One day Ali Baba was cutting wood in the forest. He saw a troop of men on horseback approaching. Ali Baba thought these men were robbers, so he climbed a tree to hide.

Ali Baba counted 40 men. He wondered whether this could be the band of Forty Thieves he had heard so much about, the dread robbers that all of Persia feared.

Their leader dismounted and stepped around a bush toward a large rock wall. The powerful man faced the wall, and Ali Baba clearly heard him shout, "Open, sesame!"

A door opened in the rock wall!

The door revealed a secret opening to a cave. The leader of the thieves stepped in, and the other robbers followed him.

Ali Baba waited until the thieves filed out from the cave. The Captain closed the door, saying, "Shut, sesame!" Then the thieves rode away.

When he was sure they were gone, Ali Baba stepped toward the rock and shouted, "Open, sesame!" And the door opened for him just as miraculously as it had for the Captain of Thieves.

Ali Baba stepped through the threshold to find a large room, filled at every inch with all sorts of valuables, so brilliant with gold, silver, and jewels that Ali Baba had to squint.

He feared the robbers might soon return. He quickly gathered as much gold as he could carry. Ali Baba remembered in his haste to say, "Shut, sesame!" when he left the cave.

Ali Baba did not notice that a single gold coin dropped from his cloak to the base of the bush that covered the secret door. Fortunately for Ali Baba, the thieves did not notice the coin that day, or the next day, or for several days, until a few weeks later.

The Captain of Thieves caught sight of the coin glimmering in the sunlight one day. He was very angry.

"How could you drop this and risk revealing our hiding place!?!" the Captain shouted at his 39 robbers.

"But, Master," the thieves said, "we know the punishment for such mistakes is most severe. Surely none of us has done this."

"Then we have been found out," the Captain growled. He paced for several minutes with the thieves waiting anxiously for him to speak. Then he announced, "We must learn who is newly rich in the town. That man and all his family must die."

By now Ali Baba had opened the shop of which he'd always dreamed. He was a fair and generous shop owner. He was happy, his family had plenty, and every neighbor was his friend.

Ali Baba hired a helper named Morgiana. She was a very clever and beautiful young lady. She enjoyed her work at the shop. And Morgiana cared for Ali Baba and his family very much.

One day, a stranger came calling at the shop. He asked Morgiana many questions about the owner, Ali Baba. The odd stranger's questions worried Morgiana. She vowed to keep a watchful eye on the shop.

The stranger was really a thief in disguise. The thief returned to the robbers' cave to report back to the Captain. "His name is Ali Baba, Captain," said the thief. "He lives behind his new shop in town. He was a poor woodcutter only a few weeks ago."

"Go back there at nightfall," the Captain ordered. "Mark his house with this white chalk, and later, I will take 20 men to the marked house and finish him."

As he was told, the thief crept in the shadows to mark Ali Baba's home. Little did he know that clever Morgiana had spotted him. As the thief marked the door, she followed with white chalk, too, and marked all the doors.

When the Captain and his 20 thieves arrived later that night, they found every door was marked. They did not know which house to attack, so they crept away in shame.

Their leader was angry and said, "Who will get this right?"

One brave thief stepped forward.

"Here is some red chalk," the Captain offered. "Mark the door, and I will lead 30 men to storm Ali Baba's home."

The thief did as he was told, but again Morgiana played her trick on the Captain and his 30 thieves.

The Captain decided to use all his power against Ali Baba. The Forty Thieves gathered together and made a plan. The Captain would disguise himself as an oil merchant. He would lead a train of mules that carried 39 barrels. The thieves would hide inside the barrels and await their Captain's signal. It was a great plan.

Early that night, they arrived at Ali Baba's shop.

"I have brought some oil to sell at market tomorrow," the Captain lied. "But tonight I need a place to stay and I have a lot of cargo. Will you take me in?"

Ali Baba was as generous as usual. "Of course you can stay here," he replied. "Leave your cargo in back. There is hay there for the mules. Then come in for dinner."

In the yard, the Captain whispered to his men, "Wait until you hear my signal. Then, leave your barrels and storm the house."

Morgiana helped Ali Baba's family feed their guest. She thought it strange that a man would arrive so early for market, but the oil merchant seemed very polite.

After everyone had gone to bed, Morgiana finished cleaning up. Her lamp ran out of oil. She thought she'd have to finish cleaning in the dark until she remembered the barrels of oil in the yard.

She walked up to a barrel. A voice whispered, "Is it time?"

Morgiana sensed danger. She answered, "Not yet, but soon." Then, gathering some hay around each barrel, Morgiana lit the hay with a torch. The 39 cowardly thieves coughed from the smoke. They popped out from their barrels and ran away to keep from getting burned.

The Captain of Thieves made his signal, but none of his men moved. Something had gone wrong again. The Captain returned to the cave to find his 39 robbers gone. Now on his own, the thief decided he would have to use all his cunning to plan his revenge. It would take time, too.

The Captain dressed as a shop owner, went into town, and took up lodgings at an inn. He opened a shop across the road from Ali Baba's shop. The Captain lived as Cogia Hassan for many months. He waited in this disguise until just the right moment.

After a while, Ali Baba invited the newest shop owner over for dinner. Cogia Hassan graciously accepted and brought a basket of fine goods. He smiled as he met Ali Baba and his family.

Despite his politeness, Cogia Hassan carried a dagger in his cloak. The blade was intended for Ali Baba and his son.

Morgiana saw the dagger first. She then recognized the man as the oil merchant who had threatened Ali Baba's household.

Morgiana quickly came up with a plan. She wore long, flowing scarves, then entered the dining room to dance for the guest.

Morgiana danced close to Cogia Hassan. Stepping behind him, Morgiana wrapped the scarf lightly around his arms then pulled hard. He could not move.

"What are you doing?" Ali Baba cried. "This man is our guest."

"He is your enemy," she explained. "He has a dagger!"

At that, Ali Baba's son seized the dagger, and the Captain of Thieves was sent directly to prison.

"I owe you my life, Morgiana," Ali Baba said. "Please marry my son and join our family in name as well as deed."

Morgiana agreed and they celebrated with a splendid wedding.

Loyalty

Morgiana, who worked for Ali Baba, was very loyal. She helped Ali Baba and his family over and over again, although she was not a member of their family. She knew that she couldn't let something bad happen to people who always treated her with kindness. Ali Baba always treated her as a member of the family, and, in turn, she was loyal to him.

Loyalty is being there for someone and helping him through tough times. It's showing that person that you will stand by him when others have turned their backs. Have you ever heard someone described as "loyal"? What made that person loyal?

The Nightingale

A Tale of Friendship

Adapted by Lisa Harkrader

Illustrated by Robin Moro

Many years ago, the emperor of China lived in a palace that was surrounded by beautiful gardens. Visitors came from all over the world to admire his silk draperies, exquisite vases, and rare flowers.

But after the visitors toured the palace and gardens, they wanted to see more. "Don't let our trip end," they would say.

A fisherman heard these words. "I can show you the most beautiful thing in all of China," he would say.

He began leading visitors into the forest to see a beautiful nightingale that lived there. At first the visitors would grumble. "We trudged all the way out here to see a plain gray bird?"

But then the nightingale would open its mouth. Its voice was pure and strong. Its song was lovelier than anything the visitors had ever heard.

Best-Loved Children's Stories

The nightingale became known as the most beautiful thing in China. Everyone had heard of this remarkable bird. Everyone, that is, except the emperor and all who lived in the palace. Even the Japanese emperor wanted to see the nightingale.

The emperor summoned his prime minister. "Have you heard of this beautiful nightingale?" the emperor asked.

"No, Your Excellency," the prime minister said.

"The emperor of Japan arrives in two days," the emperor said. "He expects to see this nightingale. Search until you find it."

The prime minister searched every inch of the palace. But he could not find the nightingale.

Now there was only one day until the Japanese emperor arrived. The emperor was worried. He summoned the prime minister and all the palace guards to find the bird.

The prime minister and the palace guards searched every inch of every garden, but they could not find the nightingale.

The next morning, the emperor of China summoned the prime minister and all the lords and ladies of the court.

"The emperor of Japan will be here today," he told them. "You must find me this magnificent nightingale."

The prime minister and all the lords and ladies of the court trekked into the woods. They were about to give up when they came upon the fisherman. He led them to the nightingale.

The prime minister and all the lords and ladies of the court marched into the palace as the Japanese emperor arrived.

"So this is the famous nightingale, the most beautiful thing in all of China," said the emperor of Japan. "I must say, he looks rather plain."

Suddenly, the nightingale opened his mouth. Out came the most beautiful song anyone had ever heard. The emperor of Japan was speechless. The emperor of China cried tears of joy.

"I must find a way to thank you for allowing me to hear your nightingale's song," declared the emperor of Japan. "He truly is the most beautiful thing in all of China."

Day after day the nightingale's song filled the palace. People crowded in to hear the beautiful music. Someone always said, "Too bad the plain nightingale doesn't look as lovely as he sounds."

The emperor heard these comments, which made him very angry. The nightingale's song had brought him such joy. He was happier now than he had ever been. "I will not have people saying unkind words about the nightingale," he said.

The emperor gave the nightingale a golden perch to sit on.

One day a present arrived from the emperor of Japan. "I hope you enjoy this gift," wrote the Japanese emperor. "It is a small token compared to the great joy you gave me when you allowed me to listen to the nightingale."

The Chinese emperor opened the package. Inside was a replica of the nightingale, encrusted with emeralds, sapphires, and rubies. On its back was a silver key. When the emperor wound the key, the mechanical bird began to sing one of the nightingale's songs. The bird did not sound as lovely as the real nightingale, and it only sang one song. Still, the emperor was pleased.

He ordered a second golden perch to be placed beside the first. "Now you will get some rest," he told the nightingale.

The people were thrilled. "Finally!" they said. "A nightingale that looks as lovely as it sounds."

They didn't notice that the jeweled bird's song was not as sweet as the real nightingale's song. They asked to hear the new nightingale over and over. The people ignored the real nightingale, so he flew home to the forest.

Only one person noticed that the nightingale had gone—the emperor. He missed his friend deeply. "Perhaps it's for the best," the emperor said. "The nightingale will be happier in the forest."

The people never grew tired of the mechanical bird's song. The mechanical bird played over and over, day after day, until one morning, with a loud twang and a pop, it stopped.

The emperor shook the bird. The prime minister wriggled its key. The bird would not play. They called in the watchmaker.

"A spring has sprung," the watchmaker proclaimed. "I'll fix it, but you'll have to be careful. Only wind it on special occasions."

The emperor was sad. He missed his friend the nightingale. Now even the mechanical bird was broken. The emperor grew sick and weak. The prime minister and all the lords and ladies of the court tried everything, but nothing helped. The old fisherman heard of the emperor's illness and told the nightingale.

The nightingale flew straight to the emperor's chambers. He perched on his bed and began to sing his beautiful song.

The emperor opened his eyes. "You came back," he whispered. Tears of joy streamed down the emperor's cheeks.

The nightingale sang a sweet song for the emperor. The two old friends visited late into the night. The emperor sat up in bed and the color returned to his cheeks. The nightingale loved the emperor because the emperor appreciated him just as he was. The emperor loved the nightingale because he was his companion.

Friendship

The emperor of China found more than just a beautiful voice in the nightingale. He also found a good friend. Nothing could take the bird's place, and the emperor was sad and lonely without him. The nightingale was a true companion to the emperor. He sat by his bed and sang and listened as the emperor talked about his troubles.

Sometimes we make friends in the most unlikely places. The emperor never thought about the nightingale being his companion until he was gone. Whom do you consider your friend? Would you miss your friend if he or she went away? What would you miss about your friend?